Death's Intern Derrick

Becky Franzel

Aw Shucks! Publishing LLC

ISBN: 979-8-9875535-2-7

Book Cover by Rebecca Richitt

Illustrations by Rebecca Richitt

1st edition (Limited Print Edition) 2023

For Jake, who is no longer here to read this.

As Erykah Badu once said under completely different circumstances: "I guess I'll see you next lifetime (no hard feelings.)"

(I told you I'd write it, didn't I?)

Chapter 1

"We need to talk."

Ericka was a tall, thin woman with a long, angled face marked by perpetual disappointment. Though only age 30, her features pulled downward by the sheer inevitability of, well, everything.

Her hair, usually tightly wound into a bun, cascaded into a series of disheveled strings. Her posture signaled urgency as she let out a bellow that surprised even herself.

"NOW," she said from somewhere deep within her stomach.

Some of her disappointments were valid: capitalism, the world becoming hotter, and the fact that she's here, in Schuester, as a glorified receptionist at a franchise nobody's heard of, at 30 years old. The prime of her life, wasted in a town with a population less than her Minneapolis high school's graduating class. If you consented to this life and if this is what you were looking for, that's fine. But if not? It's hell.

It's not really my place to say which of her disappointments weren't valid. As Ericka knows too well, the world never feels like a kind place when you haven't found your home, and it's hard to find positives in a place you feel you don't belong. Even if you seem to have everything together on the surface.

But today? All of her disappointment and frustration was 100% valid, objectively.

Ericka had been waiting outside of her boss Harold's door for this effect, surprising him as she had been surprised by the headline of the daily newspaper, *The Schuester Stories,* that she held in her hand. The headline that made her spit her coffee out this morning, not figuratively but literally, all over the otherwise immaculate white circle coffee table in her kitchen. All over the burro plant that she considered her pet, one she monitored as a helicopter mom would monitor her child.

Then, there was the email from a higher-up. Subject line: "What are we doing about this?" Label: *high importance*.

The right foot of her block heels made a *thud* as she tapped it on the checkered, cream-colored carpet, expectantly, though it wasn't done intentionally. A nervous tick. The thin floor muffled the sound slightly yet still held each beat that hung as Harold absorbed what was being thrust upon him at that moment.

A Tuesday morning.

Ericka's boss, Harold, was a short and heavy man reaching age 70, with a round face defined by perpetual discomfort. One that seemed to be constantly sighing because the weather was too hot, the traffic was too congested, or the neighbor kids left their bikes on the sidewalk again.

Unlike Ericka, none of these disturbances were quite so existential. Harold was born and raised in Schuester and had bought a house on the same block he was raised in with his high school sweetheart, Cheryl, who was exactly two weeks younger than him. He never had any other job, any other love—they wed when they were 22—any other way of life. He didn't care to. This lifestyle might sound like hell to some of you. But if it's what you want, then it's a paradise.

Or a relative paradise, at least. He would have also been fine with an actual paradise—a beach somewhere sipping on a salt-rimmed margarita with his wife, Cheryl. Where that beach would be, he had no idea.

He was comfortable, and anything that disrupted this constant state of comfort he treated as a personal assault. Not that he would take it out on anyone, but he was not one to stay quiet when facing any discomfort, big or small. This usually manifested as a sigh, a groan, or any other similar vocal drag.

Harold groaned, an empty coffee cup in his hand, looking at the actively brewing Mr. Coffee 12-cup with a lustful longing before looking to Ericka.

“Excuse me, what?” Harold asked, looking at her from underneath his disheveled brow, as if in afterthought. A gesture that signaled this—whatever Ericka was complaining about—was secondary to his own personal distress.

Ericka raised her brow as she rose a paper newspaper in her right hand, pointing at the front headline with her left index finger.

It would be a lie to say she hadn't been waiting for this, as if the words weren't hanging on the tip of her tongue expectantly, ready to fall all at once from her mouth.

“Have you seen this headline?” She jabbed at the paper again for effect.

Harold sighed and paused to read the headline. He looked at Ericka, then at the headline, then at Ericka again.

"DEATH, INC. EUTHANIZES PEOPLE."

“Ericka, it's not that bad—”

Harold had seen the headline. He, too, got the paper. He, too, read it every morning. But, unlike Ericka, he had grown accustomed to the news' fluctuations—the bad would always even out with good, eventually. What seemed catastrophic one day would even out by heroic firefighters saving a cat from a tree, or something akin to that. The natural order.

At least, that's what he told himself each time someone brought up global warming or systemic issues or student debt, or anything else that made him uncomfortable—things he didn't have answers to.

It will sort itself out

was an unproductive stance in the face of complete helplessness he felt within his soul when confronted with complex problems.

It will sort itself out

seemed like the best answer, at least for his personal and mental well-being. No further thought required.

And he knew Ericka would react this way, but before he could finish his thought, Ericka interjected.

“Harold, did you actually read the article? I mean, did you really read it?” The loose strands of hair she had tucked behind her ears fell around her face. She enunciated each word carefully, precisely, to ensure nothing got lost in translation, as it often seemed to do around here with her.

Harold leaned into the paper Ericka held up. Looked again, harder, putting his face closer to the newspaper, as if there was something he maybe missed. Maybe he overlooked something.

"DEATH, INC. EUTHANIZES PEOPLE."

“Well, it isn’t too far from the truth. I mean, it’s not completely accurate, but what news corporation is?” Harold asked.

“Did you keep reading? They know where we’re located.”

Harold leaned in again, squinting his eyes to show his focus.

Suite #6 in a private office complex between Main Street and Surrey Ave has been a mystery to us, a reminder every year when the lease is renewed in September that we have no idea what actually takes place there, but the lights are always on. A town mystery.

That mystery is no longer shrouded, no longer in the shadows. Now we know, but the reality is much worse than what we all pondered behind closed doors.

Not a butcher. Not a puppy mill. Not the holi-

day cake shop that is open year-round despite no known customers. (We're still actively working on this case. For more information, see p. 5C.)

They sell death.

Harold laughed. "Oh, my. That's just 100% flat-out wrong. We don't sell death. Death happens, whether people like it or not."

"Keep reading," Ericka said, an implied sigh hanging after her response. Clearly, this was his first time truly reading it, rather than simply skimming the headline.

"Just because they're scared of death, doesn't mean it's wrong. It just *is*. Death is inevitable," Harold continued as if he were commenting on a golf game—calm, cool, collected. "I don't know how many times we have to explain this."

"Harold, please just keep reading. HQ already emailed me. Our jobs are on the line here, and last I checked, we don't have any sort of severance pay." This time, it was more imperative.

He continued where he left off.

According to local resident Marian Witherspoon, former Death, Inc. secretary—

Then, he stopped and looked up.

"Oh, dear. Not Marian. . ."

Honestly, Harold should have known. Marian, their office secretary, left on less-than-kind terms only two months ago.

Not that any of that mattered now.

Harold continued reading Marian's quote.

> *—said, "I am not joking when I say they have a LIST of who to save and who to kill. DEATH!! Their salaries are paid to choose which souls pass onward!! Souls that could still be here TO-DAY!!"*

"She never really fit in with us, did she? A bit dramatic. . ." Harold looked to Marian's headshot in the newspaper—it was smug, chin and nose turned up, as if she were about to say, "White after Labor Day? Really?"

"Did you hire her, or did I?" Harold asked Ericka, honestly not remembering how Marian got there in the first place. It was as if she had shown up one day, ready to work, and no one asked questions.

Ericka looked visibly distressed. Her sleeves were rolled up unevenly on her striped, white-and-navy H&M blazer, staring at the headline again as if she had misread it. As if, perhaps, she was in the wrong.

No. Ericka knew exactly what they did. And while it wasn't problematic, there was a reason she never told her dates what she did for a living. There was a reason she kept it vague—"an executive assistant", she'd say—when they would press her. Something she had heard her business major brother say once. While her job was necessary, it wasn't something people understood easily. This newspaper headline could kill them, at least metaphorically.

And she remembered Marian. She remembered that, while Marian left dramatically, and while Marian was a bit insufferable, she wasn't entirely wrong. What Death, Inc. did was morally questionable.

Ericka didn't think she was overreacting here.

Harold persisted. "Ericka, we've been through this before. We'll deal with it again. The public's attention span is just so, so short. We just have to wait it out."

She looked up at him. *Again? Again?!*

“How many times has this exact thing happened?” was the only thing she could think to say, filtering out expletives and additional one-word questions, like coffee grounds through a sieve. She tried to temper her tone and keep it professional, but it came out terse.

Harold looked to the ceiling and counted inside his head, then double-checked by whispering and counting with his fingers.

Harold assured, “It’s probably happened 10 times—”

"10 times?” Ericka's voice went higher, thinner. She turned her head and ran her hand through her already-askew black hair, her ponytail disassembling more as her face visibly dissembled with every new bit of information. Her face melted as she looked back at Harold in disbelief.

“So, we're saying this has happened 10 times in this same town? You’re saying something like this has happened 10 times?” Her voice grew softer as it became harder to control her tone, as reality sunk in.

Harold continued as if Ericka hadn’t said anything, “In the same town over the past 60 years, give or take.”

“So, we're saying this has happened once every six years?” Her voice's pitch grew higher in an attempt to keep herself from yelling.

“Give or take,” Harold said calmly, without notice to Ericka.

Distracted. He was distracted. This was in the middle of his coffee time.

He always had his coffee at 9:00 am sharp, right after he arrived at the office.

Harold looked over Ericka’s tensed shoulder at the coffee pot that had just finished brewing, now sputtering and steaming.

He was sure someone else would be circling in soon enough—the caffeine vultures that inhabited this office, no doubt. It looked like Susan. Blonde-bobbed Susan, head of New Beginnings, formerly Life, Inc., formerly Soul Savers, and so on. She was like him in that she was always on her way to get coffee or coming back from getting coffee, but different in a way he couldn't place. Perhaps in that she cared more? Or maybe she spoke more? Or maybe it was the bobbed haircut?

Either way, knowing Susan, the pot would be gone, and he'd have to brew an entirely new one. Hardly a good use of his time. *What, with his meetings, his crosswords, his. . .*

Ericka interrupted his trance.

"Harold, we can't do this anymore. The internet will remember this. It's stuck, now. And people will remember. People can link back to it and be reminded. It's not like it used to be. Listen, please listen to me. Even in six years, things have changed so, so dramatically . . ."

Harold looked over Ericka's shoulder, and Ericka grabbed onto Harold's. She shook him once as if to shake the cobwebs that seemed to linger over his eyes when he so transparently didn't care about the world outside of him.

"Harold, did you hear me? We can't do this anymore. What if something like Reddit sees, and it just keeps coming back?" She wasn't even sure if Reddit was popular anymore, but it was the first thing that came to mind. If they got ahold of it, it would leave some footprint.

"Who's Reddit, now?" Harold asked, wondering in the back of his mind if Reddit was a journalist his father had slighted. He was never great at keeping track of that stuff, but usually, he didn't have to. Usually, this stuff would pass unnoticed. A blip in the collective consciousness.

But if Ericka was this concerned, maybe he should be a bit more concerned. Ericka was generally a bundle of nerves, but usually, she could be assuaged. Or at least, after this much time, she'd come up with a solution of her own. And if HQ was already emailing about it . . .

Finally, Harold said, "But if it would make you feel better, yes, we can work on our image. It's probably about time we updated it—yes?"

Ericka sighed a breath of relief. "Yes, that's what I'm saying. Yes. We need to do something. And I think this would be a very good start, a good st—"

"An intern," Harold interrupted. "Maybe a marketing intern from the local community college."

"An intern? Don't you think this requires a bit more intervention? Maybe even a marketing agency? PR? Something?"

"That's not in the budget."

Ericka sighed. "Okay, sure. An intern will be fine, but it will require more work on our side. Are you okay with this?"

"Of course," Harold said, mentally putting those tasks on Ericka's plate as he returned to his computer.

Harold opened his local Craigslist to create a listing.

"Local business looking to hire a—"

No, we're not a local business. We're a franchise, Harold reminded himself.

"Great opportunity for growth for a young marketing—"

No, not that. Too scammy.

"Marketing professional needed." Brief, and not promising anything he couldn't deliver. No lies. He never mentioned they didn't have the money to pay. And he never mentioned what they'd need the professional for—just that the person was needed.

The cursor blipped. Words did not.

Harold thought about what was most important to him in a candidate, and he couldn't help but picture exactly what he disliked about Ericka.

It wasn't like she was terrible. She was an excellent employee. He liked her as a person.

She lent them extraordinary processes. She was organized. She was never late. She never let her personal life impact her work life.

But it was inevitable, as much as he tried to keep it from his mind. He tried to keep that negativity out of his mind these days, as he was reaching retirement, and he had read a

Web MD article about how negativity was bad for your heart health. Or something like that.

Time. Ericka always wastes my time.

Not on purpose, but with. . .well, the work. The work that could be brushed aside. The meetings that could be dismissed. Harold didn't want someone wasting his time. The emails she forwarded over and over and over, waiting for a response that he didn't have. Not because there was no response, but because he genuinely didn't care enough to respond. Why couldn't she just be cool and let it go?

No, that was never in Ericka's constitution.

With that in mind, Harold added detail to his listing: "Please only call between 10:00 am-1:00 pm."

He looked to his answering machine, still cassette recorder. The cassette was full.

He added, "Do not leave a voicemail. We will not listen to it."

He read it through once more, thinking if there was anything else he should add before publishing. That had to be it, right?

They needed a marketing professional. Check. Right in the heading—the most crucial part.

He would not answer their calls anytime outside of 10:00 am-1:00 pm. *Check.* He couldn't even if they tried, even if they were able. His cassette was full. And even if he cleared it, he probably still wouldn't check his answering machine or call them back. That's how it got full in the first place. He didn't have that time on his hands—not at this physically wearied age and temperament.

Before Harold could even second guess himself, he hit *publish* and filled out the next form, wondering if he should add anything else with no intention of going back to edit.

reply

Marketing Professional Needed (Schuester)

Please only call between 10-1.

Do not leave a voicemail. We will not listen to it.

555-781-1323.

- do NOT contact me with unsolicited services or offers

Chapter 2

Derrick was sitting in his apartment on the other side of Schuester, on the side furthest from the highway in a studio apartment he moved into when he moved back from NYC. That was six months ago. He had gotten by through a series of temporary jobs and remote contract work, but barely. His bank account took a beating after his three-month data entry contract was cut short, and his English major credentials screamed "But what are you doing with your life *existentially* speaking?" every time he looked at his sunken face in the mirror.

He moved back to his hometown here, a place even his parents got out of as soon as he graduated high school. Not because he wanted to move back, but because living here was affordable—a global pandemic made his former Brooklyn apartment uninhabitable and impractical, and he was trying to tackle the surprising amount of student loan debt he found himself in.

That didn't mean he didn't want to live here. It was a fine town. There was plenty of space to exist. He found a coffee shop he liked that wasn't a Starbucks. But that didn't mean he didn't *not* want to live here. It's just not exactly what he envisioned. No high rises. No exciting parties rubbing elbows with elites in Los Angeles, in New York City, in Atlanta. No running into exciting opportunities by pure stupid luck simply by being in the right room, as he had hoped for himself before the world was upended.

He wasn't sure what he wanted anymore, so he found himself in the holding cell that was this indecision. Everything that had seemed so certain before had shifted and morphed into a parody of what had once been.

He didn't know where he wanted to live. He didn't know what he wanted to do. Hell, he didn't even know if he was overthinking it or not thinking about it enough.

Much like in his earlier years, when he played the trumpet for far too long just because he couldn't choose a better instrument to play, he found himself waiting for an outside force to intervene and make the decision for him. Now, he was too tired to make this choice himself. The indecision was exhausting, constantly battering the sides of his brain as he tried to consider his options. He longed for an adult to dictate his next move for him, with a promise of success on the other side. No more uncertainty.

This didn't mean he was complacent—not that. He could usually find something interesting about anyone or anywhere he chose to go, could find meaning in what others may find none in. Some called it optimism, but maybe it was something more than that.

Or maybe it was something less.

Who's to say.

Still, he oscillated on whether he'd like to be here in 5 years, in 10 years, or maybe 20. Would he be able to find happiness here? Would he find the success he was hoping to achieve in this lifetime? What about love? Can you fall head over heels in love in Schuester, or do you settle?

But now, in this very moment, that wasn't what was on his mind.

Even if he wanted to leave, there was nothing he could do, unless he was going to be very irresponsible about it. In his teens or early 20s, maybe he would have left with $20 in his pocket. But now? At this very moment, the only thing on his mind was his rent—due five days ago.

And while his financial situation wasn't catastrophic yet, he wasn't sure when it would be. He kept his "rent due" notice on top of the bills pile, sitting on his end table, wilted, like the saddest stack of pancakes. He could have his electricity shut off and survive, at least for now. Water would suck, but he would get by. But a roof? He needed a place to stay.

He opened up Craigslist.

He had been on all of them—LinkedIn, Indeed, ZipRecruiter—but they didn't provide the instant satisfaction of "to hire immediately, no contract required."

Craigslist was the home of one-sentence job descriptions that could mean, "This job doesn't entail anything else other than this one sentence" or, "Shit, I don't know what this job is, but we need someone to do all of the things."

In this moment, this was a gamble Derrick was willing to take.

He hovered his mouse over the headline: "Marketing professional needed."

That one sentence. That was all. No all caps. No dollar signs. Just exactly what he'd be able to get with his degree, or at least he thought.

He had seen so many of these postings, and usually, none of them meant what they said. He scrolled back up and clicked on it.

There was nothing in the body, outside of a phone number with the aside "Please only call between 10:00 am–1:00 pm. Do not leave a voicemail."

Calling? Still just calling? No emailing? Not even a voicemail?

Derrick couldn't remember the last time he made a phone call, but that's probably why he didn't have a job. *Phone phobia.*

He looked down at his phone, a four-year-old Google Pixel with two elongated cracks through its screen making an ominous *X*, a screen he was sure would shatter irreparably if he dropped it once more.

Call. He should call, right?

He looked at the ad again.

reply

Marketing Professional Needed (Schuester)

Please only call between 10-1.

Do not leave a voicemail. We will not listen to it.

555-781-1323.

- do NOT contact me with unsolicited services or offers

Surely, it was a trap. But surely, he'd be able to discern if he just made the damned phone call.

But what if they were good at lying—like, *really* good? What if it put him more in debt, somehow—taking this job?

"The people who get fucked with the most are the ones who are already fucked to begin with. The ones who are most likely to drown are the ones who are already in the water," Derrick remembered his grandpa saying, or something like that, from a reclining chair well past its expiration date, littered with cigarette burns.

That was Grandpa Al. Maybe he had said it nicer, but that was doubtful.

Grandpa Al never said these things like there was anything you could do about it, or any sort of actionable lesson, some cautionary tale. It's just the way it is—unavoidable. Shit's fucked. You have no meaningful sort of agency. That's the way life is sometimes, according to Grandpa Al.

And Derrick knew he was already in the water—unable to see what was a life raft that he could use to paddle to shore, or what was milfoil tangling around his leg and keeping him under.

But even as he was thinking this, he held his phone in his hand. Ready to dial.

The number was already entered. All he had to do was press *call*.

It was 10:01 am. Was it too soon? Or was that the exact type of punctuality they were looking for? Or was 10:01 am too late? Were they looking for someone who would call exactly at 10:00 am, or does that show the prospective employee is too punctual, inevitably insufferable?

He couldn't even look up the company because they hadn't even put the company name in the description. Glassdoor couldn't help him now.

But perhaps they couldn't provide that information. Perhaps it was top secret, he thought.

Perhaps they'd pay him top dollar to keep their secret, while only expecting menial labor from him—his true calling in life. He could keep a secret if they paid him well. How deep of a secret, he was unsure. It'd have to be case by case, he assumed. Covering up murders could be acceptable if he was making six figures, probably, but if it was in the high fives?

Difficult to say, unless he knew the details.

10:05 am.

But what could I do for $20 an hour? He wondered. That was the more realistic question he should be asking himself. While Schuester was as nondescript a town as you could find—probably the best place to commit a large corporate coverup undetected for decades, if you really wanted to—they weren't looking to hire someone off Craigslist for this.

Derrick was drowning, but he wasn't a fucking idiot. As fun as it was to think they were hiring a Bond-style spy with payment of ultra-secretive high figures, he knew that this job was probably not that.

Or maybe that's what a fucking idiot thinks to himself. Who's to say.

It was 10:06 am when Derrick finally pressed *call.*

Chapter 3

Harold rested his chin on his left fist, his right hand gripping an old fountain pen hovering over a yellow legal pad. He wasn't planning on writing anything, but as people passed by his office, he wanted to look busy if anyone decided to peek in. Busy, but not anywhere near his inbox, to account for the emails he was actively ignoring.

He was sitting on his particle board desk, painted an imitation cherry wood color rather than stained. His brow was furrowed, pupils resting just below them looking through the porthole window on his door, and he watched people pass his office in twos as they hurried to their next meeting.

One he was late for. Or rather, one he was actively avoiding.

10:01 am.

It was another meeting with HQ—something they were trying to mediate between Death, Inc. and New Beginnings. Harold wanted to avoid that as much as possible. Like the plague. He was never good with conflict. That was always Ericka's strength, he justified. Might as well let her run with that one.

And it wasn't like he was missing much. These meetings happened frequently, as Death, Inc. and New Beginnings tried to work their processes together seamlessly—a Herculean task for the two vastly different corporate cultures.

Death, Inc. and New Beginnings were technically run under the same umbrella company, if you could call it that. It's difficult to tell who was truly running things here. Even those who had been with the company weren't entirely sure who ran what, or who was on top. But technically, if you were to look at the legal paperwork, it was two branches under the same company, name unknown. Both processes were necessary for the other to function, in the way that a battery needs two electrical charges of opposite polarity to work.

It made more sense when it was Death, Inc. and Birth, Inc. Showed what they did more clearly. More straightforward. One created the processes for life to begin. The other created the processes for life to complete.

And New Beginnings could have stayed with their original name—Birth, Inc.—but they always had more of a start-up feel. Perhaps it comes with the territory of working with the beginning moments in life versus the end stages, but they had changed names six times in 60 years, and rebranded more times than anyone has the desire to tally.

To be clear, New Beginnings and Death, Inc. didn't always exist. They were created as a natural answer to a man-made problem that the modern funeral industry created. As the funeral industry started using formaldehyde to preserve bodies at the turn of the 20th century, souls did not naturally pass as they had before. More ghosts. More specters. More poltergeists haunting their favorite mortal abodes, begging for release.

There were several theories as to why this happened, by the nation's top philosophers and biologists—the souls could not pass when the body was not decaying, the souls reacted to the chemicals as they hung around the body postmortem, or perhaps something entirely different.

Several theories, no definitive answer.

Death, Inc. stepped in during the 50s to create a process to manually pass on and recycle this soul, stripping the individual mortal experiences from the blank-slate soul itself. While there was no way to strip the soul completely, not entirely, it was a nearly flawless process created over the past half-century.

Not much is known about the original owner of Death, Inc. other than he was a former mortician turned psychologist who happened on wealth midlife, seemingly by chance. He created Birth, Inc. to complete the process. Or at least that's what he said publicly.

Some said it was a way to distribute his funds across companies, but that is also simply theory.

As time passed, souls in the United States had evolved to depend on these services, meaning they were no longer able to pass themselves on to their next living corpus. When Death, Inc. removed and recycled the soul from the deceased and wiped its memory, Birth, Inc. picked up the recycled soul and assigned it to its proper fresh inhabitant. The souls waited to be processed, compass broken, completely reliant on their shepherd to guide them to their proper new home. If they weren't reclaimed, they would simply absorb back into the body until finally processed.

Death, Inc. and New Beginnings mostly dealt with humans, but in the past five years, they had recently started working with animal souls in the past five years because of the recent uptick in pet preservation, as well as poisoning, contaminated water, and so on.

While technically, Death, Inc. and New Beginnings were under the same company, their divide seemed greater based on their vastly different corporate cultures.

Anyway, back to the meeting Harold was late for—something about the exchanging-of-souls process they had to diagram. Apparently, there had been a mix-up. A human soul was assigned to a newborn chickadee's body.

Death, Inc. had filed a soul incorrectly, apparently. Allegedly. That was according to New Beginnings, at least, who was never shy about placing blame before all the evidence was in. However, how this happened, nobody seemed entirely sure. Several theories, no obvious answer.

To: Harold@deathinc.com
Subject line: To whom it may concern,
Message: See below.

Objectively hilarious, Harold thought, but apparently, New Beginnings didn't think so.

A human soul in a chickadee's body didn't seem too bad, at least not in Harold's mind.

Probably for the best, Harold thought, though he'd never say it out loud. Being a human, with human responsibilities, is a lot of work.

In a grass-is-always-greener, rose-colored glasses mentality, the chickadee seemed to have forgotten how awful human responsibilities are, and how blissful life could be without a mortgage.

But maybe it didn't know that yet—the human soul inside the chickadee's body. Though it was apparent its memories were not completely wiped clean, even if the only evidence was that it still knew how to spell "HELP." This meant that this soul didn't complete the entire soul-cleansing process that was supposed to occur when a departed soul is entered into Death, Inc.'s system. This means that either they never received the soul due to technical issues, or that the soul was received but not entered in their system.

Or maybe, it was some issue that would surely be above his pay grade.

Harold had heard of experiments done in HQ—transplanting unwashed souls into animal bodies—but those were phased out, at least officially speaking. He had heard of the fringe groups, too, the ones Marian connected with online that expedited her departure, but those were typically in Minneapolis, Chicago, and Los Angeles. Not here. Not Schuester. They weren't active here.

The phone rang, a sharp, sudden sound that jolted him from his thoughts. "Hello, this is Harold," Harold answered, grateful for the excuse to miss this meeting. A gift from Heaven, if you believe in that kind of thing.

Though Ericka looked into his office pointing at her wrist—the universal motion for "it's time!" Harold now had an excuse. He welcomed the call. He pointed to his phone resting on his shoulder, shrugging while mouthing, "Gotta take this," exaggerated lip motions to really convey what he was saying.

Ericka gave a thumbs up, but with a stern face. She tried to hide the snark, no time for that. And she should have expected this would happen, honestly. This meeting was now her total responsibility, as it always ended up being, somehow—some way.

But on the other end of the line, silence. Harold repeated himself, "Hello, is anyone there? Harold speaking." The dead silence continued for a beat before the other caller began.

"Hello, Harold. This is Derrick." *Act confident*, Derrick thought.

Harold furrowed his brow, thumbing through his mental Rolodex of names and faces he knew. *Derricks. Derrick. Any Derrick.* Anywhere?

"Do I know you, Derrick?"

"I'm calling about the job you posted on Craigslist," Derrick said.

Of course, Harold thought. He had only posted it two days ago, but he had nearly forgotten it, chalking it up as a loss. Young kids not wanting to work, or something like that. He hadn't thought it through. Only in small, passing moments, when he felt a primal desire to be angry but had no ready outlet.

"Ah, yes. The marketing assistant we've been waiting for. Thank you for your call, Derrick. You know, we've had a lot of interest in this role!" Harold lied as he watched the meeting room's door close, making eye contact with one last coworker before it shut for the last time. Safe. "Say, Derrick, why don't you tell me about yourself."

Harold wasn't sure what he should be looking for. He had never worked with a marketing assistant in his life. They never had to market. Why would they need to market? They rarely face the public. They had to exist, whether people liked them or not.

Nevertheless, Harold continued when there was a dead silence on the other end of the receiver. A silence that he knew wouldn't end on its own volition. He'd have to help it out.

"Like, for example, where did you go to school to learn that marketing, or what makes you think you'd be a good marketer?"

"I went to school for English," Derrick said.

Harold was impressed, though for misguided reasons. "So, English is your second language then? I wouldn't have been able to tell if you hadn't said anything, but now I think I'm picking up a bit of an accent, Derrick. You speak it well, though."

"It's my native language, actually. I studied English writing and rhetoric, actually, so a bit more in depth than just learning to speak it, actually," Derrick assured as he coiled his black hoodie string, frayed, around his pointer finger as he spoke until it nearly cut off his circulation.

But Harold wasn't listening. Ericka was pounding on his door. Though he didn't know it, HQ was demanding that he be in this meeting. Not even for his expertise, but just to check the box to say they had spoken to him. Ericka had tried to get past it, but they insisted, so now, here she was—insisting because of an insistence.

The door was locked, so Ericka jiggled the handle. If there had been a doorbell, she probably would have rang it repeatedly.

Harold looked at the door, furrowed brow, visibly annoyed. He waved his hand to Ericka, in an attempt to dismiss her. She knocked again, mouthing, *Now, please*

Sigh Harold thought before he continued on the phone.

"You know what, Derrick? Why don't you tell me about it in person. Face to face," Harold said without asking Derrick to repeat himself. While Harold hadn't heard what he said, Derrick's tone sounded confident. It sounded like a definitive answer. He was willing to give him the benefit of the doubt that it wasn't something dumb, horrific, or overtly racist.

"That sounds wonderful" Derrick paused, searching for more words until he finally landed on "Great."

"Come in tomorrow and we'll discuss. We have a lot of work for you to do, but I still want to be sure you're the right person for the job. Okay?"

"Of course. Do you have an address?"

"Address? Yes. It's 142 Goulding Ave. Next to the highway. The only building on the block. Can't miss it. Tell the front desk you're there to see Harold. Okay. I've got to go. You got that?"

"142 Goulding Ave. Next to the highway. Tell the front desk I'm there to see Harold."

"There you go." But instead of a goodbye, there was a *click*.

Derrick was about to say he was looking forward to it, but before he could, he heard a click from the other end.

Sigh. Derrick was about to say he was looking forward to it, but he wasn't sure whether to celebrate or worry. Whether to lose sleep preparing or to rest for a day filled with surprises.

Luckily, that was his coping mechanism. As soon as he was stressed, he was tired. As soon as he was overwhelmed with stress, he was also overwhelmed with exhaustion.

So he slept. He slept until he woke up at 9:00 am and realized he had never made a time to meet at the office. They hadn't told him on the phone. He checked the Craigslist post. He had no idea.

I could call them and ask. But would that have to be in the timeline they set, between 10:00 am and 1:00 pm again? Would that be too late? Was he already late?

Derrick pulled out a pair of khakis he bought for his previous job, the data entry job that turned out to be remote—he just sat at his home office all day in sweatpants, despite their oddly rigorous dress code. He pulled those out, noticing they were stiffer than he remembered. They had a firm crease from other pants piling on top of them, the fold line accentuated.

He didn't have an iron, so he tried to flatten out the crease with his palm. But there was no use. *Maybe it would be fine*, he thought. Better than showing up too late. But was he late?

He was getting tired again. The exhaustion.

He thought about making coffee, but that would take too long. He thought about grabbing some at a drive-thru, but who knows—what, with the world the way it was, the ecological crisis causing coffee prices to rise, not to mention the overwhelming guilt associated with drinking a beverage made from a bean that was endangered, or at least close to it. Not to mention, they were often harvested by people who were paid far less than what they were worth—no matter what advertising campaigns would try to lead you to believe.

A shirt. He would need a shirt.

A white button-down was all he had, short-sleeved. It was cold, but it would have to do. He threw a black hoodie over his outfit to wear from his car to the office. Not something he would wear inside, of course, but something to keep him warm and comfortable in the interim. He ran his hand over it, noticing the pills in the cotton rising above its fabric line.

It's fine. It will do.

He looked up the address on his phone, noting the time and mentally pairing it with a song of nearly the same length.

It would probably take him around 15 minutes—what, with the stop lights, the four-way stops, the rigorously enforced 15 mph speed limit through half of his commute. He scanned his playlist in his head for 15-minute songs. Jimi Hendrix's Voodoo Chile would probably cut it. The droning sounds acted as a meditation that started as soon as his key turned in the ignition, easing in with the bass, then keys, then drums as Derrick's brain focused itself on thinking about nothing at all—on turning into a calm, blank slate.

Chapter 4

142 Goulding Ave. An office building. Industrial. Cheap.

But how had I not seen it before? He thought to himself. *And why were there so many old Buicks in the parking lot?*

142 Goulding Ave, the only building on the block, as Harold had said on the phone the day before. The lights were off on one entire floor, the third floor—but every light was on in the first, second, fourth, and eighth.

Curious.

Derrick got out of his '98 Honda Civic and locked its door, though he wasn't sure he needed to. It didn't seem anyone else would be here. Still, the habit was a good one—never heard of anyone regretting they locked their car, have you?

The sidewalk was overgrown with crabgrass and dandelions that had crawled their way through the cement crevices, then wilted as summer closed. It was autumn in Schuester, now Mid-October.

Derrick didn't mind the overgrowth. In fact, *the less concrete, the less developed, the better*, he thought. This was one of the reasons he convinced himself he was better off not living in New York City anymore—not enough nature. He would never see this happening in Times Square. Here, nature found its way without being plucked from the ground from which it miraculously spawned.

Derrick shoved his hands into his hoodie pockets—though it wasn't cold, even for October. It was out of habit. A nervous habit. He never knew what to do with his hands, so he hid them. He's done this for as long as he could remember, always making sure he had pockets in his wardrobe to accommodate for any sudden anxieties that may come his way.

He tried to open the door, a glass door, black metal handle, but it was locked. He tried the door next to it—another glass door, black metal handle. Locked. He tried the first door again. Locked.

Then, a voice. A woman's voice from a speaker next to the door.

"Are you here to see Harold?"

Derrick wasn't sure if he was supposed to answer, or where he was supposed to direct the sound to whom he was speaking.

"YES!" Derrick shouted, like your elderly grandmother shouting into the speakerphone when she calls you.

"Beautiful. Derrick, I assume?" the voice said as the door clicked open. "Harold has been expecting you."

As Derrick walked in, he wanted to ask if he was late, but figured that would show a lack of confidence. He didn't want to appear any less confident than he already was. He needed this, but he didn't want them to know how *badly* he needed this.

"Good morning, Derrick. My name is Anissa. Would you like me to take your hoodie?" the woman at the front desk asked, but in a way where there was only one answer—*yes*.

Derrick took his hands out of his pockets and handed it to her reluctantly, relinquishing his safety blanket. "That would be great, thank you."

"No problem." She took the hoodie and folded it seamlessly as she walked with the effort of a seasoned retail worker. The last time it had been folded, rather than balled up and thrown in the corner, was questionable.

"You're going to want to take the elevator to the eighth floor, then turn left. Harlod's office is a few doors down on the left. You can't miss it, but of course, let me know if you have questions or if you get lost when you're up there," she assured.

"Sure thing" Derrick said, walking toward the stairs.

"Good luck."

Derrick looked at her for a moment. *Good luck? What did she mean by that?*

As if she had read his thoughts, she continued, clarifying, "Not that I mean anything by it. Just felt right to say."

"Oh, yeah. Thanks," he said, finally looking her in the eyes. Or rather, looking at her right eye, noticing the scar that ran down her right brow and through her cheek. He tried to smile naturally, without drawing focus to the fact that he had noticed. He nodded as he continued. "I appreciate it."

"The scar? Yeah, it's a brutal one," she acknowledged. "Don't worry about it. The interview. I'm sure you'll do great."

Derrick turned toward the elevator to avoid continuing the conversation. He knew if he continued speaking, it would continue to be awkward. He nodded toward her in the unspoken gesture of saying *thanks again* and continued to the elevator, where his thoughts spiraled as soon as the doors shut.

He cleared his throat before the doors opened, revealing the eighth floor's hallway. A long hallway with a 1990s-style short carpet—one that seemed to cling to and repurpose any crumb that fell on it. He saw a door at the end of the hall on the left.

On that door was a placard, hung askew, as if he had hung it himself, or perhaps bumped it and never got around to fixing it. *Harold Whittier.*

Derrick could feel his mind turn, beginning the overthinking wheel—the negative thoughts, the panicked thoughts. *You should have brought your resume, Derrick. You should have worn something else. Khakis? What are you, a missionary? You should have brought him coffee. Buttered him up a bit.*

But as he stood there at the other side of the door, Harold had already seen him through its porthole window, gotten up, and opened the door for him.

Chapter 5

"Ah, yes. Derrick. Welcome. Come on in. Sit down. I see you didn't bring any coffee," Harold began.

Derrick's face turned white. "I know, I should have brought some—" He tried not to fidget. He tended to wring his hands when he was nervous, a telltale sign that only led him down a further spiral. Instead, he gripped his waist with his hands, focusing their energy.

"That's not what I meant," Harold laughed. "What? No. I wasn't expecting you to bring me coffee. I was saying you didn't bring any for yourself. Would you like some?"

Derrick consciously relaxed his shoulders.

Harold continued. "It's not like it's the best coffee in the world—makes Folgers look like some fancy indie bookshop's local blend, if you know what I mean. But, well, sometimes that's the stuff that actually wakes you up, isn't it?"

Derrick laughed thinly, and nervous, yet he managed to say, "Sure, I'll take a coffee. Thank you."

"Cream or sugar?"

"Just black."

"Well, to each their own." Harold said with a raised brow, as if Derrick's coffee preference was an affront to him personally. He looked at Derrick, now sitting in the chair across from Harold's desk. Derrick was a good 40 years younger than him, but older than he thought he'd be.

Derrick noticed there were crumbs on Harlod's table—so many crumbs, but no food. Harold saw him notice and brushed them onto the carpet to the left of his chair.

". . .Would you like me to get the coffee?" Derrick said, unsure if Harold had briefly forgotten.

"No, no, no. I've got it. You wait right there, and I'll be right back," Harold said as he got up to walk toward the coffee pot that was in the open common room kitty-corner from his office. Kitty-corner enough where he could keep an eye on the coffee pot, but not so much that people were staring into his office.

There was a line—of course there was a line—but Harold didn't mind. This time, at least. He needed a moment to think things through. How he'd go about this.

He knew that Death, Inc. didn't have money to give Derrick a good salary. Nothing that would make him comfortable.

You barely know him, Harold. Maybe he's living with his parents and truly just needs the experience before he moves on.

Nonsense, Harold. No parent in their right mind would let their child go to a job interview in a short-sleeved button-down shirt and wrinkled khakis.

What to do.

"I see you have a bite," Ericka said from behind.

"Excuse me?" Harold jumped, startled by Ericka's voice.

"The kid in your office. He's been fidgeting in there for the past 10 minutes. What did you say to him? He looks genuinely scared."

Has it already been 10 minutes? Harold thought, looking at the people in front of him having a conversation in front of the coffee pot instead of pouring anything.

And, usually, this would have upset him. Susan and her assistant, Denise—they were always blocking the coffee pot, not noticing the world around them.

But today, he didn't have time to stay mad. Today, he had something. Harold nudged them lightly, edging his way between the two oblivious barriers between him and the pot.

"Did you hear me? I asked what you said to him. He looks like you told him his grandma died or something. . ." Ericka paused, visibly recalibrating. "You didn't tell him his grandma died, did you?" suddenly serious.

"He came in that way. A little jittery, but seems like a good kid." Harold ignored her second question.

Ericka leaned into Harold, using a ventriloquist-like mouth to mutter, "I mean, he seems really nervous. Why is he so nervous?" as if Derrick was watching them and could read lips from 30 feet away. Her lips were smiling, but her words were concerned.

"Don't talk so loud. He can probably hear you." Harold looked over his shoulder as he said this as if checking to make sure the kid hadn't flinched or turned his head at his name.

"Either way, Harold. I'm worried he might be *too* nervous."

"I have a good feeling about this kid," Harold said, and he did. That was the truth. Nerves were a good thing. That meant he wasn't going to come in here with an attitude. That meant he was open to learning—he wasn't taking in what he's learned from other jobs and trying to impose their standards here. Blank slate. "Nerves are a good thing. Better than not caring."

"Maybe you're right," Ericka said.

Harold nodded, unnecessarily sage. "I know."

Ericka moved past it. She was used to Harold adding unnecessary weight when he dictated even the simplest of his thoughts. "I've got the hiring paperwork in my office, if you need it. Let me know when you'll need it, if you think he's a good fit."

"Of course."

"And we should probably talk about that chickadee situation—"

"I've got my plate full at the moment, Ericka, but I'll help you as soon as I'm done." Harold hoped that would keep her at bay for a while. She was always better at dealing with those situations, the soft negotiations, the problem-solving. That had never been his strong suit. A chickadee leaving desperate cries for help on their doorstep was definitely more under her skill set, not his. He'd never been good with customer complaints.

Ericka sighed. "I'll forward you all the emails they're sending me. I need you to have my back so if you could reply all saying you stand by what I'm saying—"

His eyes went blank again. *The only way she'll learn leadership is if I let her handle these things on her own,* he justified.

Harold walked with two coffees toward his office, where Derrick was sitting in a leather chair across from Harold's desk. His arms were lightly touching the armrests as if they were delicate, as if he was scared his arms would collapse them. Hovering, slightly.

Derrick leaned forward to grab the coffee from Harold, and Harold sat down slowly. Derrick crossed his legs, the tip of his shoe scuffing against the face of the desk.

Silence.

"So, do you start, or should I?" Harold said.

"Excuse me?"

"I suppose I should start, shouldn't I? I guess that's the natural order of things, isn't it? I ask the questions, you answer them. Then, the tables flip—you ask, I answer," Harold pontificated, buying time. Time bought, still no answers.

Derrick looked to Harold for another moment of silence.

"So, what makes you interested in Death, Inc.?" Harold finally said.

"Death, Inc.?" Derrick repeated. It was at that moment that Harold realized he had never told him the company name. Had never told him what this job would entail outside of the vague *marketing professional.* Didn't realize how this might sound after last week's very public news.

"DEATH, INC EUTHANIZES PEOPLE."

Harold looked back at him and shrugged.

Derrick continued, visibly flustered. "I'm sorry, I want to be clear. This is for a marketing professional, right? Not a mercenary?" Again, Derrick didn't think a mercenary was below him if the pay was right, but he wanted to know what he was getting into.

"What? No. No, no. Nothing of the sort. Unless you mean killing it with words," Harold winked, to signify he was using a pun. This felt unnatural to him, which showed transparently on his face.

Derrick stared back at him, blank. Still contemplating how much per hour he'd take as a mercenary—how much was suspect, how much was insulting.

"No, Derrick. To be clear, we do not kill people at Death, Inc."

Derrick thought back on the newspaper article he had seen the week before.

"DEATH, INC EUTHANIZES PEOPLE."

Derrick thought to himself, *Well, that explains why they need marketing.*

"Was this role created for the newspaper article that was published last week?

"That was a misunderstanding," Harold spoke over Derrick's last syllable.

"I never said it wasn't, but I'm just trying to understand what this job—"

"You can't believe everything you read, Derrick," Harold assured. "For starters, I think I was pretty clear that we need a marketer—not a mercenary. I said that right in the post. I wouldn't lie on the internet," Harold said with a definite tone that he wasn't sure was true. He had never lied on the internet, no. But he also didn't use the internet often, so he wasn't sure if that made him less credible.

"What would I be marketing? Death?"

"You're not marketing death. No. Of course not. You're marketing, well . . . what we do here. The natural process of easing the process along. The soul side of it—allowing a soul to complete its journey from death to life. You'll respond to these allegations and make us look good, so they know we don't go around killing people," Harold said casually, sipping his coffee.

Derrick sipped his coffee, then took a deep breath, looking to Harold. Harold crossed his legs, bumping the bottom of his desk with his knee.

"What do you mean by that?" Derrick asked, this time not aggressively, but apprehensively. "Marketing a peaceful transition, I mean. I'm still not completely understanding, if you don't mind me saying. Will I be doing PR?" He knew he needed this job. He wanted to believe it was a real one. Was ethical. He wanted to believe this job could work.

Harold's computer let off a *ding*. An email. He looked at it, looked at Derrick, then looked at his computer screen. "Well, what if I show you? That way, you can decide for yourself," Harold said.

Derrick paused. What he was about to see could be the thing that convinces him to take this job. Or it could be the horrific aftermath of some crazed madman given carte blanche.

Or maybe something in between, Derrick assured himself.

"We don't have a ton of time—so either you're coming with, or I'm going to have to excuse myself . . ." Harold paused to explain. "With our dealings, our deadlines aren't exactly manmade, if you understand what I'm saying. There are some things that need to be done in the immediate, or things will go . . . well, not entirely as expected."

"Sure."

Harold stood up. "Great, great. Follow me. We have to go into the basement and make sure things pass on as expected. Then, we need to file the printout in the correct file folder, otherwise, things will go . . . well, again, not entirely as expected." But the way he said it was uncertain, as if he, himself, was unsure what would happen if they were late.

"Sure," Derrick said before he could process his words, out of body.

He assumed he'd understand better once he saw it. He assumed it'd either make him feel better, or it would make him run. Either way, it would be definitive.

Harold turned right out of his office, down the hallway, and to the stairs. He caught Derrick paused in front of the elevator and explained.

“No elevator. If it breaks . . .”

“Breaks?” Derrick asked, wondering if that happened often.

Harold ignored his question. “If it breaks, things will not go as expected.”

Harold pat Derrick on the back, which made Derrick jump. Unexpected. A misplaced gesture in an undefined moment.

Harold didn't notice and continued his thought. "Why don’t we just work down there if it’s such a time crunch, you ask? Well, I like a window, and this thing’s in the basement.”

“Sure.”

“You sure say *sure* a lot.”

“Sure,” Derrick said again, before correcting himself. “I mean, I guess.”

“Follow me,“ Harold said as he pushed open the door to the stairwell.

Derrick followed Harold down the first flight of stairs, the second flight, and the third. On the fourth, they got hung up by Susan and her assistant Denise from New Beginnings talking and taking up the stairwell, so Harold blurted out some pleasantries to announce his presence.

“I’m sorry. Excuse me. Great weather. Yes. We’ve got to go.” Harold repeated this as he wedged his way through them, then rounded the corner toward the fifth flight down. He started complaining about gatherings in the stairwell around the sixth descent, muttering, “They could literally talk anywhere, but they always choose the stairwell or the coffee pot.”

When they reached the seventh descent, it became markedly darker. No more windows. Several more stairs, and they were eight floors down. The basement.

“You usually will have no reason to go into this room unless we’re really overwhelmed, or if we need you for backup,” Harold explained.

“Backup?” Derrick asked.

"No time," Harold said, though he could have easily explained himself as he made his way toward an outdated-looking machine, colored blue. A large, square-foot block with register tape spitting out the top, whose sole purpose seemed to be spitting out a number. *9-2-1-3-7.*

9-2-1-3-7, Harold muttered each number to himself after he ripped off the register tape, then moved two steps to the right and reached for a folder furthest to the left. He didn't look up once, as if guided solely by muscle memory.

"9-2-1-3-7," he said as he opened the first folder. He pulled out a piece of paper, then ran his finger down a list of numbers signifying a list of names. Three columns of numbers paired with three columns of their corresponding human's names. He scanned the left column first, then the left middle, then the right middle—until he found the number *9-2-1-3-7* in the right middle, near the middle of the column. "Aha! Found ya, 9-2-1-3-7, Harvey Nelson," Harold said as he closed the first folder.

"Is the list they mentioned in the newspaper article?" Derrick asked.

Harold didn't respond.

Instead, he continued, pulling out another folder, next to the previous folder further to the right, set out as if it were part of a prepared process—like a sous chef's mis en place before a Saturday night shift, each piece a necessary component. Each piece placed for maximum efficiency. Not a thing out of place.

Harvey Nelson. Harold muttered to himself. *Harvey, Harvey,* Harold said as he looked down the sheet. *Where are you—aha! Harvey Nelson. Soul Signifying Number: 9-2-1-3. 9-2-1-3 Harvey Nelson. 9-2-1-3."*

Derrick asked, confused, "So, what part of the—"

"No time for that, now—I'll explain later," Harold said as he typed *9-2-1-3* into a different square-foot block, one that looked nearly identical to the square block that initially spit out the number. It was green rather than blue, and it had a sticker on the side—faded, amorphous, the silhouette of a bulldog.

"What's the purpose of those two machines? They seem pretty similar—almost like we could combine them, no?"

Harold shot a look back at him, as if to say, "That's just not the way we do things around here." He offered no further explanation.

"You're right, I'm sorry," Derrick said, though he wasn't sure why he was apologizing.

"It's very important that you don't touch either of those machines unless you have to pass someone on, do you understand?" Harold said. "And don't ask me any questions about them because, well, I'm not about to mess with a good thing. It's Ericka's project, and you know how she gets about these things." Harold paused to give Derrick a knowing look, and Derrick tried to give the emptiest look back to him. Of course he had no idea how Ericka "got about these things". He didn't know her.

"One moment." Harold went backward through each of the files he referenced. He picked up the second folder, then crossed out a line. He picked up the first folder, then crossed out a line. He then stapled the receipt paper to another piece of paper that held rows of other receipt papers, filling the page like rows of tassels on a highly stylized country artist's vest.

"This is how we know what year the death happened in," Harold said, raising the page but offering no explanation on the rest of the process. He set this paper in a third folder.

Derrick started. "When the what—"

"Excuse me—I've got to finish this," Harold interrupted as he picked up a beeper and typed something in.

"Couldn't this be automated?" Derrick asked.

"No," Harold said, not even a pause for thought. He closed each of the folders, flipped a switch on the first machine, picked up the third folder, set it in an "outgoing" countertop filing cabinet, then swiveled toward Derrick. "See? It's that simple. Barely an inconvenience."

Derrick nodded. He had many thoughts, but he allowed his head to nod up and down rather than to continue to probe.

I'm still interviewing, he thought to himself. *I'm still interviewing.*

Harold backtracked. "Or not you, I guess. You're in marketing, or PR. Hopefully we won't need you in here at all, but it's always useful to have you understand the basics. Or, actually, we could probably use you, if you're up for the challenge. . ."

Derrick noticed a fourth folder, black, significantly better kept and newer than the other folders. Unlike the other folders, it did not clearly have a place. Harold saw Derrick noticing it and put it under the table. Not an elaborate hiding spot—but clearly, a hiding spot.

Harold saw Derrick noticing the folder, and tried to stay ahead of it.

"Oh, that? That's not important. Don't worry about that." He waved his hand in the direction of the folder, as if to brush it off.

But before Derrick could ask Harold anything, Harold had already started walking toward the door.

"Let's finish your interview, yeah?" he said to Derrick over his shoulder.

Chapter 6

"You passed that one on, right? I'm guessing, but would like to confirm," Ericka asked Harold as soon as he got upstairs.

Rather than answering, Harold motioned toward Derrick. "Ericka, this is Derrick. You will be taking him for the second part of his interview."

"But Harold, I have a meeting in five minutes."

"I'll take care of it," Harold said, though he had no idea what the meeting was for or what it would entail.

Ericka raised her brow.

Harold nodded, definitively.

"Hi, Derrick. Nice to meet you," Ericka said, still looking at Harold, as if trying to solve a puzzle.

It wasn't an important meeting—nothing that would do much to damage if it didn't go well, or if he was woefully unprepared. It was a weekly accountability meeting with HQ that he technically should have been a part of all along, so perhaps this would turn into a good thing.

"If you're willing to handle this meeting, I'm thrilled to take over the interview." She smiled at Derrick, as to finally acknowledge him.

Why is Harold passing off the interview? Derrick wondered.

Why am I passing off the interview? Harold wondered. It seems like the right thing to do. He'd seen it done before. It seemed right, somehow. A confident act. As if he had some sort of process in place where there was none.

"Nice to meet you, Ericka," Derrick said, a bit late—but better late than never.

"Pleasure is mine," Ericka said as she still maintained eye contact with Harold.

Why is he passing off the interview? Ericka thought.

"Follow me. And bring a chair, please," Ericka said. She pointed to a break room chair near them, plastic, no armrests. Light. Perhaps she'd keep the chair her office. This would be an upgrade.

Derrick grabbed the breakroom chair. When he lifted it, it jerked up and hit the bottom of the table it was tucked into, lighter than he expected. He then followed Ericka into her office.

Smaller than Harold's, but not by much. Hers was two offices down.

"Have a seat," Ericka said as she motioned toward an empty plot of carpet on the floor.

"So, what brings you to Death, Inc.?" Ericka asked as she folded her hands on top of her desk, maintaining eye contact.

"Honestly, I'm not entirely sure," Derrick said, before he could stop himself. He shifted in his breakroom chair and paused. "It's not that I don't like the job. It's just . . . I'm not sure what the job is. I'm not sure I understand what you're doing or what Harold is doing, to be honest."

This is why he passed Derrick off to me, Ericka thought to herself. Yet another task that he dug into and couldn't climb out of. Now it was her turn to figure it out.

She looked down at her papers—the hiring documents that Derrick would presumably need later that day, unless he really screwed things up.

She looked up.

"Our goal is to organize souls into their proper categories. After death, it is our job to . . . well, allow the soul to pass on to its next living journey. To make sure there isn't as much pain after the heart stops beating, if this makes sense." The only way this made sense to her is because she grew up around it. She grew up knowing it and understanding it. But when she tried to explain it to her friends, partners—anyone?

She was usually met with the same exacerbated look Derrick now held in his eyes.

"We do not intervene until the natural end-of-life processes have taken place, to be clear. We step in once the body ceases to function and releases the soul, to be clear. We do not intervene before that happens. Only after."

Derrick had many questions, but the first one that fell out of his mouth was "I'm just confused on the machines. The number. The folders. It all seems so . . ."

Shit, Ericka thought. *Of course he's overwhelmed.*

"Harold showed you the recycling room, didn't he?"

"I think—"

"The room with the folders and machines, downstairs. The basement room with no windows."

"Yeah, we just got back from there."

Ericka sighed. Of course he wouldn't understand yet.

"Ignore all of that."

Now, Derrick looked back blankly. Ericka panicked at his lack of reaction—much more unsettling than either overwhelmingly positive or negative.

"Or maybe, don't ignore it. We'll explain it eventually, but it's not something you need to know now, is more what I'm saying. It's nothing illegal, at least. There is nothing illegal about what we're doing, which I feel like I need to make clear based on—"

She wasn't sure how she was going to finish that sentence. *Based on what?* Their work was something outside of the realm of everyday life. Something no law touched on. Laws are for the mortals. Death, Inc. deals with the step after mortal. One step past what was their shared familiar. She cleared her throat.

"Well, Derrick, based on the idea that our company often gives. I'm sure you've seen the news lately. I'm sure you've seen the stories."

Derrick's leg shook, concentrating his anxieties.

"We'll tell you what all of that was downstairs soon enough," Ericka said, looking at Derrick's leg, then back up to him.

Even if he could solve *some* of their problems, or even be another voice of reason, that would do. Her life would be so much easier if there was just one more logical voice of reason in the room.

But she couldn't show that. She knew she couldn't let him know that. She cleared her throat and corrected her posture, leaning over her desk.

"So, what makes you think you'd be a good fit here at Death, Inc.?"

Derrick tried to shake himself out of his frozen state. He had a sense of "I've got to have this job" paralysis, looking a job he didn't trust dead in its eyes as he leaned in to kiss it.

"I graduated with an English degree two years ago, and I have been gainfully employed ever since." His voice was monotone, but his leg wouldn't stop shaking.

"Impressive," Ericka said. "Do you have a portfolio?"

"No," Derrick answered too quickly. *Shit.* He course-corrected. "But I'd be willing to do a writing assignment, if that works for you,"

Ericka leaned in, eyebrow furrowed, and said, "Yeah, that might work better, actually. Right?"

Derrick still looked back blankly, but inside his mind, he was panicking.

He knew he needed this job. He knew it. He was going broke in his childhood hometown, late on his bills in an apartment where you could literally smell the mold as soon as you walked in, never mind seeing it.

All the red flags were there, yes. He could see them as clear as day.

But now? Maslow's hierarchy of needs was kicking in. Security over morality. First, he needed security, then he could worry about morality.

He needed an out. He needed to get back on his feet again. He needed anyone—really, anyone—to give him money.

At least for a little while. At least until he caught up on bills, until he refreshed his wardrobe, and had a bit of time to save some money. Then, he could get out.

"That was rhetorical, to be clear," Ericka said as she saw his panic. She sat back in her chair, and crossed her legs and her arms over her chest. "I think that should do fine. How would you feel about writing us a press release to give back to us next week? Is that okay?"

"Sure," Derrick said, knowing he could look up how to do so. Knowing it couldn't be too difficult. *Right?*

Ericka paused. "Or, we could just hire you now. Lord knows we need you, and we could use all the help we can get at this point."

"Excuse me?"

"How does $20 an hour work for you? Benefits included. Starting tomorrow?"

Derrick couldn't believe it. "That works for me," he said, concealing his shock at finding a job that wouldn't make life a struggle for once. One where he could start saving and planning for the future. Maybe moving up. Maybe moving out. And maybe getting comfortable, in the meantime.

Ericka said nothing. She immediately picked up the phone and said, "We hired him, Harold. He'll start tomorrow. I'll have him complete the paperwork. If you could enter him into the employee directory, that would be great."

She laid the phone down. "I told Harold you got it. Now, if you don't mind, there is some paperwork for you to fill out. Nothing too complicated, but let me know if you have questions as you go through it." She opened her laptop and escaped into a world of tasks behind her screen.

Chapter 7

Anissa, Death, Inc.'s secretary, was on the other side of Schuester when it happened. A triple-car pile-up, 5:25 pm. As everyone was coming home from work, Anissa included. She was the middle car.

The other two cars? Life-threatening injuries. One DOA. Cars completely totaled. But Anissa?

While she was hurt—her side throbbed—her injuries were not life threatening. There was nothing she could really do but stay still and wait out the pain. Maybe a concussion, a few bruised ribs, which was a damned miracle based on how her own 2012 Toyota Yaris looked. Like a crushed soda can. Absolutely totaled.

Overall, the paramedics said she'd be fine. And they asked her if she wanted to go to the hospital, but she knew she'd be fine if she didn't. She'd rather not spend the money. She knew how to mend herself at this point. At this point, it was old hat.

This was not unusual for her. And it was not as settling or as ego-boosting as you might think it to be, at least not for Anissa. For her, at this point, it was unnerving.

She's had 16 near-death experiences. At only 30 years old, 16 of those aren't just a miracle. It's suspect.

If there was any god up there, she suspected they were trying to kill her. Or maybe they were toying with her, like a cat does a mouse before it goes in for the kill. Scaring it and batting it around a bit before pouncing, ripping its head off one final time.

At this point, that's the only explanation she could come up with. It was her running theory for the past 10 years of suspect incidents, where she should have died—where everyone else under the same circumstances had passed, but she had not.

Sure, she didn't live a careful life. Not in the slightest. And to be fair, the other instances were far more her fault—this one was an anomaly. The free climbing incident went awry when she climbed too high while alone, vacationing in Hawaii's Oahu. And an incident when she was camping in the same spot as a black bear and her cubs while she was in northern Wisconsin.

And she had the scars to prove it.

One long scar down the right side of her face, for starters—a thin yet prominent line from her right brow to her right cheek. That didn't come from the bear's claw, mind you, but from a branch that caught above her brow then dragged down her face as she was running away. It was hard to miss that one. That one, she was proud of, though it was the hardest to cover.

The others were easy to hide, but not this one. This was one that seemed to startle any paramedic that came to the scene after. "Well, Ms. Fontaine, luck certainly isn't on your side, is it?"

That is, if the paramedics didn't already recognize her, either from interacting with her before or from the newspaper articles.

"Anissa Fontaine Dances With Death" was the most recent headline, where she fell out of a tree—her favorite tree in her parents' backyard, one she had never fallen out of before, but the branches aged as she aged and inevitably snapped. And there she went. Down. Fall. *Splat.*

Scientists have contacted her asking if she'd like to participate in a study on mortality, but she said she'd rather not. But they kept calling. She stopped answering as soon as she began to recognize the numbers.

At this point, it was embarrassing. She didn't want all her near-fatal mistakes known to the world, but all you had to do was Google her name. The problem with living in small towns, as she had for most of her life, is that it was harder to fade into the background.

Her business was everyone's business. And somehow, the word always got out beyond those small town's borders.

"We meet again, Ms. Fontaine," a familiar-looking paramedic said as he arrived on the scene, though she couldn't place his name. *Thomas, maybe?* He stepped over a piece of glass from the windshield of the red Toyota Corolla that ran into the bumper of her Yaris as he walked past her.

This "We meet again, Ms. Fontaine" —this paramedic's voice rang in her head as her friend, Gary, drove her home in his '82 Volvo back to the place she shared with Gary and his partner, Stephanie. Not because Anissa couldn't afford her own place, but because it seemed easier. In case something happened. In case there was another injury. She was only 30, but she knew that if something else happened, there was a significant chance she wouldn't be able to care for herself on her own.

She moved with them from Cripple Creek, Colorado, where they were all originally from, to Black Mountain, North Carolina—to here, Schuester, when Stephanie found a good job and both Anissa and Gary followed like button quail to their new home.

"You have to be more careful," Gary said to Anissa.

"Careful with what? Driving? I don't think this one is my fault, Gary," Anissa said, looking at his profile as he drove.

"You know what I mean." Gary's face scrunched and tilted sideways.

And she did, but she didn't want to admit it.

"Honestly, Gary, I don't know what to do, not at this point."

It's not like she wanted to die, but it seemed more straightforward than dealing with the injuries, the traumas, the medical bills that she took on before she realized a hospital visit would become a near-regular thing. Now, for the most part, she's learned to mend herself. Or maybe your body becomes used to the chronic pain after you've been hurt so many times. Maybe she'd just grown used to being sore. Maybe this was her norm.

It just seemed easier.

"I didn't mean it like that," Gary said to Anissa, correcting himself while keeping his eyes on the road. "We worry about you is all. I know this luck isn't your fault."

"At least most of the time," Anissa said to lighten the car's mood.

"Yeah, I mean, sometimes, it has been your fault. Let's be clear on that. But this one? Shit." Gary ran his hand through his dark brown hair, turning salt-and-pepper colored with every day.

They don't tell you that when you're young, though you age gradually, you notice it suddenly and abruptly. Anissa looked at the hair lining Gary's temples and wondered if she had seen his grey hair before—wondered if maybe she hadn't noticed enough, if perhaps the adrenaline was heightening her senses, and she was noticing more about her surroundings. She wondered if she looked like this to other people. She still saw Gary as the 19-year-old who raised chickens in his duplex and had not one, but five, vintage Harleys he swore he'd fix once he had the money for it.

Not that it mattered. Not that she cared how she looked in other people's eyes, but she wondered if she was still seeing herself as a younger version of what she was now—the mirror a reverse Dorian Gray portrait that would always stay the same in her eyes as her face continued to age.

She was only 30 years old, for Christ's sake. But that 30 happened far quicker than she thought.

These revelations occurred more as more things occurred, as if fate were dialing things up a notch—her near-death experiences became more frequent, each one more random and different from the last. As if her life was on a strange repeat. She couldn't predict it. Even when she was trying to be safe, it was like as if there was an anvil perpetually hanging over her head, the rope unraveling from the pressure of the anvil's weight—not quickly but creeping, snapping each fiber until only a single, stubborn thread remained to hold it up.

"Have you thought about getting health insurance, Anissa, or are you still against that? I really think at this point, you should at least consider it. I mean, Christ, look at you. I would like to take you to a hospital without bankrupting you."

"Not much they could do, anyway. I'd just be paying a copay for them to say I should rest at home. They'll say there's nothing they can do. Maybe they'd give me an alcohol swab and a Tylenol. Nothing you can really do about ribs."

"You say that like I should know that from experience, but you realize most people don't have that experience, right?"

"Well, you're welcome," Anissa said.

"Yeah, well, you know. We just want you to be well, Anissa. It's like you've got a shadow on you, or something. But we're always there for you, okay? No matter what."

"I appreciate that, Gary. I really do. I hope you know that. I know it can't be easy, but I'm incredibly grateful."

The near-death experiences began when Anissa was around 20. A whitewater rafting excursion on the Colorado River, where she and her boyfriend at the time went on a solo trip with not enough training and too much alcohol.

He did not make it out alive. His body was mangled between two blocks of granite bounders. The current smashed his body against them again and again and again, and his body could not get over until the water finally carried it over with its current.

She was conscious enough to call for help once she got to shore via her emergency GPS, but she passed out after that. She couldn't even remember the paramedics showing up. All she could remember was a slow descent into her unconscious, then waking up in a hospital bed with an IV in her arm and a pounding headache. She was in the hospital for one week, and the bill nearly knocked her out again.

Six years after the first accident, she went for a hike where she slipped down a cliff and broke her arm. *Another miracle you're alive,* the doctors reminded her, before saying *you really should be more careful.*

Two years after her hiking accident, she slid down the stairs with a glass in her hand. The glass shattered into small yet daggered pieces, stabbing her as she fell. Glass shards through the front of her torso. This wasn't like Hollywood, where you can just roll through glass unscathed. Real glass doesn't cut like Hollywood's sugar glass.

Gary snapped Anissa out of her flashback, back into the present with a sigh.

"Yeah, well. It's the least we can do," Gary said, patting her shoulder softly without taking his eyes off the road.

Anissa relaxed in the passenger seat of Gary's car as much as she could. Adjusting when she felt a stab of pain—readjusting when she felt another stab of pain. Until finally, somehow, someway, she fell asleep. The sunset peeked under the sun visor of the passenger's side window as she sunk herself into the headrest.

Chapter 8

Derrick didn't expect to be back so soon. He assumed there would be some sort of vetting process, some sort of deliberation, even if it was just to keep up appearances. But maybe that's how it works sometimes.

Right? That's how it works sometimes? He questioned as he opened the heavy-glass front door, now unlocked as he waved his new keycard in front of the electronic lock.

Anissa was sitting at the front desk again—bandaged, but well, considering her accident just the day before. She held her torso but still insisted on doing that oh-so-typical half-walk, half-jog toward him, the one everyone does when they want to get your attention but don't *really* want to hurry. Though she was in immense pain, her furrowed brow intensified every time her left leg hit the floor. She was cradling her side with more intensity each time that happened.

In her right hand was his hoodie, and she held it toward him as she said, "So glad I caught you. You forgot your hoodie here yesterday."

He left the day before in a haze. An employed haze, sure. And yet, a skeptical haze. An "it surely can't be this easy" haze. He held photocopied paperwork in his hand confirming his employment for a corporate job. One that seemed. . .something.

Today he was no less skeptical, though he was happy to have his hoodie back. He was wearing the same shirt as yesterday, a short-sleeved button-down, but the air conditioner was on high despite the October weather.

"You're going to need it," Anissa said. "The air conditioner is broken. I can't turn it off. Figures that this would happen when it's cold, right?"

"I mean, you can borrow it if you want. I'm sure I'll be moving around a lot today, and if you're just sitting there—" Derrick said, before realizing he was speaking.

Unconscious gestures. Like a courteous vocal tick. He regretted the words as soon as he said them.

"There's more to my job than just sitting there, Derrick," she said not in a mean way, but neutral. "Sometimes, I also stand up, or I turn in my chair if I'm feeling extra crazy," she added to lighten the mood.

He apologized by muttering something akin to "Oh no, no. No, no, no. I didn't mean it like that." He took the sweater from her hand and continued the conversation in his head as he walked to the elevator and pushed the eighth floor button, replaying it and creating alternate plotlines as he felt the elevator jerk up.

And when the elevator door opened, he walked out and ran into Ericka.

"You're here," Ericka said as a knee-jerk reaction, leveling her coffee cup to account for the disturbance—a small trickle down the white ceramic mug. She straightened herself up again and corrected herself.

"Let me show you where you'll be working," she continued.

She had been setting up his office since 5:00 am. She knew she'd have to get here before anyone else. That was the only way she could get his computer.

New Beginnings had recently tossed their nearly new computers, still functional. They recently upgraded to new MacBook Pros to improve morale, they said. Their Lenovos *just wouldn't do,* they said, no further explanation required. She looked at the thick hunk of laptop.

They're not wrong, she thought to herself.

Ericka had to maneuver a desk that she found on the curb around the corner from her apartment, somehow—one she had picked up for her own home when she was hoping to build a home office but ended up gathering dust and excess junk mail in the entryway of her home. Not large, but large enough to look comical with only one person navigating it.

This is a better use for it, she thought as she dragged it through the lobby. It felt like 30 minutes to go 20 feet to maneuver this desk and fit it in the elevator. She tipped it slightly on its side, but not so much that it would be too tall. She took the chair Derrick had dragged from the break room the day before, moving it from her office to his.

She was on the lookout for an extra monitor, but for now, this would do.

The setup was basic, but he'd have his own office to decorate, if he was into that.

"Nice, thank you," Derrick said as he looked around at the bare walls. He wasn't much for decorating, but he could probably put a calendar up for morale. To keep up appearances.

Ericka looked from wall to wall, trying to figure out what exactly was nice. She found no *nice* here. Only a carpet she wished she would have steamed, and dusty walls. How did the walls accumulate this much dust? She tried to look away slowly to not draw attention to it.

Nevertheless, she nodded and smiled. "We do our best with what we have."

Derrick sat down in the breakroom chair he selected the day before. He adjusted his seat within his chair, corrected his posture, and planted his feet below his knees. He set his hands on the desk, then on his lap, then back on his desk. He placed them crossed on top of his closed Lenovo computer.

Ericka noticed nothing.

"You may have noticed the laptop." Ericka nodded toward the laptop underneath Derrick's hands. "We have it all set up for you—your user name and password are on a sticky note that you'll find on the keyboard. Don't worry about getting too much work done for now. For now, we just want you to settle in and go through some of the paperwork I've left you on your desk."

"The first page is filled with a few basic rules before you get started, so you know what's happening in the office," she continued. "I figured it would be easier to print them out, so you can take notes as they change or have it on hand. Sometimes, it's awkward to ask the etiquette of an office, so I figured that would be useful."

Death, Inc. Basic Rules

1. Work starts at 8:30 am. Let me {Ericka} know if that will be an issue, and we can sort things out.
2. There is an office next to yours that appears open, but it is not. This is not free space. It is occupied.
3. Coffee is free, but we encourage a weekly donation. $5 is fine, if you're going to be drinking coffee.
4. The laptop is company property, so please always keep it on the premises.
5. Do not access work documents from your home device.
6. The landline phone on your desk does not work. Sorry.
7. Any other questions? Ask me (Ericka). If your questions are personal, please email me. Much easier.

Ericka continued. "I've also printed out an organizational chart of the people you may encounter during your time here, should you choose to stay with us. If you'd rather not, you may discard them in the wastebin next to your desk."

Death, Inc. [us]

Harold: He is your direct boss. Technically, you report to him.

Ericka [me]: The operational side of Death, Inc. I will be guiding you through the training process.

Dennis: His work will not intersect with yours.

New Beginnings [we work with them]

Susan: She is their boss. Technically, you should also listen to what she says.

Denise: She is Susan's assistant.

Natalie: Her work will not intersect with yours.

> Anissa: She works the front desk. She will be your go-to when you have questions about HR-related things, or building-related issues (e.g., badge, ID tag).
> Jared: He is the janitor. Not sure if you'll need to know him, but he's a great guy and you should say hi if you see him.

"Is the bin the Whole Foods bag?" Derrick asked as he glanced at the chart.

"Yes, the Whole Foods bag for now, until we get you a trash bin."

Derrick thought he saw someone near his door, a man wearing all black—but when he did a double take, he realized his eyes must have been playing tricks on him.

But no.

Now, he saw the reflection of a man wearing all black in the window, though quick.

Twice.

There was something familiar about him, but not by appearances. Something about his aura seemed familiar. Not warm. It was—

"Dennis, fancy you showing up today of all days. What's the occasion?" Ericka said in the figure's direction.

The figure, or Dennis, groaned. "I think you know why."

Dennis didn't visit this level often. Usually, he's out in the field or working in his office in the basement, but he was invited to a meeting about the chickadee. He was aware of the chickadee. He had flagged this as an issue—it was, what, eight months ago? But here we are, still talking about it. Here he is, still answering on it, even though there was a clear paper trail exonerating him. He made sure of that from the start.

Explicitly clear.

He wasn't sure why he was attending a meeting with the Birthing Department or New Beginnings, as they've made very clear they want to be called.

But he planned on making it a quick one.

“Hopefully it’ll be a quick one,” Ericka said in his direction, but eyes unfocused, as if her own internal thoughts were her teleprompter.

***

Only a few minutes earlier, Anissa also did a double take as she saw Dennis. Not because he looked familiar. No. His presence *felt* familiar. His eyes, knowing. They stared directly at her—an uncomfortable kind of familiar that she couldn’t pinpoint.

But from where?

“Are you hurt?” Dennis said as he looked to her lower abdomen. But the way he asked it was as if he already knew. He didn't end the sentence with the upward-questioning lilt, but with a period.

To be fair, her pain was probably obvious. She was subconsciously cradling where her ribs had been injured—probably bruised. Nothing to stay home from work on. She also couldn’t take another day. She had just started here, and she wasn’t sure how many recovery days they’d let her take.

Her mind switched to Dennis. His resemblance felt uncanny. Unsettling. Like she should know him as he seemed to know her, but also didn’t want to say anything.

“Oh no, this? I’m fine.” Anissa brushed her arm away from her torso, letting it hang by her side awkwardly. She felt more comfortable the other way, but she kept fighting the subconscious tick to return to her old position. She didn’t want anyone to worry about her. Or even knowing she was hurt.

Especially Dennis, for some reason. She especially didn’t want Dennis to know.

“Did something happen?”

“Just a car crash. I’m fine. May I take your coat?”

Dennis didn’t respond, only looked down to her abdomen again with his knowing eyes. As if he was analyzing her wound.

"Okay, well, you be well now, okay? Take care of yourself," he said before making his way to the elevator.

"Thank you. You too!" The moment she finished her sentence, she knew he was already gone.

Chapter 9

"Derrick, may I see you in my office." Harold stated this, not asked, as he leaned into Derrick's office. Surprising him. At the time, Derrick had been trying to start up his Lenovo ThinkPad. He was logged in, and everything seemed good until it suddenly turned off on him. He turned it on again, but then it turned off.

But this time, it seemed promising. A circle spun at the bottom of the screen, showing that something was happening. What internal processes were happening, who knows—but something was, indeed, happening.

"Sure, no problem," Derrick said as he carefully closed his laptop halfway. He didn't want to interrupt the process, but somehow leaving it out completely open seemed. . . wrong. He didn't know why, but it seemed wrong based on all the rules on company property.

"We have a few things you need to write, and it may have to be on a deadline. Have you gotten your computer to work?" Derrick looked back at his half-open computer, unsure if its failure was his fault, or something else.

"I can also give you a pen and paper, and you can type it out on mine. I know how temperamental those Lenovos can be. I have one myself. Isn't that one of the computers the Birthing Department just got rid of?"

"I'm not sure," Derrick said.

"Fair enough. First day. First-day blues. It happens to the best of us." Harold lingered by the front of Derrick's door, oscillating between leaning on the frame and standing in its middle before continuing.

"As we discussed before, I'm sure you saw the newspaper that says we sell death. Obviously, we do not sell death, as you can see from our operations here. Can you write something that says we don't sell death?"

Derrick paused. "I'm not sure I understand. You just want me to write a press release that says "Death, Inc. Doesn't Sell Death?" Should it come from us, or should it come from someone else?"

"What do you think?" Harold said, knowing nothing about how complicated this was. *All he has to say is that Death, Inc. doesn't sell death. That's all he has to do, right?*

"I think we should come up with a plan, first. A way to rebuild that trust we've lost—"

"But we need it now."

Derrick wasn't sure if this was the place for this conversation. He wasn't sure if he had all the details quite yet. He wasn't even sure what they did precisely, or what any sort of value proposition they brought.

"It's not going to be that easy."

"What do you mean?"

Derrick wasn't entirely sure what he meant either. He had never been in a marketing role or a PR role. The only thing he knew about marketing was from TV. Specifically, from *Mad Men*. And even from his brief view into the marketing journey, the few times they mentioned it was when men were doing "man" things and women were underappreciated and devalued constantly. Then suddenly, poof, an idea. No process. Just output.

"We should think this through together."

"I don't have time for this now," Harold said with a furrowed brow. He rubbed his temples in circular motion, trying to will some sort of thought to escape his head.

Derrick opened his laptop again to check on its progress, then shut it halfway again. He opened it again, then shut it almost all the way before he stopped himself. All nervous ticks. He wasn't sure what to do with his body. What was he expected to do in this moment?

"Ericka, can you come in here for a second? We need you," Harold shouted into the hall. Ericka opened her office door and leaned out its entrance. On her door, a sign reading, "Please Do Not Disturb" swayed, pendulum-like. The sign appeared to be stolen from The Rusty Creek Inn, a local motel about a mile away, its namesake printed at the bottom in red text.

"I'm busy," Ericka said before closing her office door behind her. The sign continued swinging until it slowed to a gradual halt.

And she was busy. Her email inbox hit 50 unread messages, all in one morning. A new record. Her job couldn't consist of missing any emails. Nobody emailed her unless they had to.

The first email read, "Re: This news article?" It was from Steven, her old coworker in Minneapolis who still kept tabs on Ericka's new office. She hovered her mouse over the email, about to click, before Harold interrupted again, insistent.

"It will only be a second," Harold repeated from his office. "We just need you to talk through this marketing thing with Derrick. Won't be long."

Ericka sighed. This was the only response she could give. She had no verbal answer to give. How she got anything done in this office was a mystery, even to herself.

She sighed, pushed herself away from her desk, and walked over.

"Hi, Derrick. Long time no talk," Ericka said in jest. They had just spoken only 30 minutes ago. Derrick half acknowledged it, when it registered to him as a joke. Ericka paused, turned to Harold, hesitant to open this can of worms. "What marketing thing?"

"Fixing this mess," Harold said in a demeaning tone, as if he were stating the obvious. He wondered if maybe he was being too harsh, but he stuck with it. There was nothing else to do. Sometimes he wondered if he was taking the right tone with his employees—whether he should be more kind and trusting or if he should take the reins.

But it was difficult to know when he didn't even know what horse they were riding on. He floundered when it came to leadership. *Any* leadership.

For that, he was lucky to have Ericka, who would always take those reins.

"Wow. Okay, this is a lot to unpack," Ericka said as she was trying to piece everything together. "We can discuss this later, but I think we need to take a rounded approach instead of a pointed one. That may be a better solution."

"I think, perhaps, I'd have a better idea of what I was defending if I had a better idea of what you guys do," Derrick said. This had been clearly on the tip of his tongue for a while, just waiting for the first open gap in the conversation to say it. When he finally let it out, his shoulders visibly relaxed.

Derrick looked at Ericka. Ericka at Derrick.

Ericka looked at Harold. Harold at Ericka.

She had planned Derrick's entire office this morning. Had gotten him a computer, had gotten him office furniture, had given him a few things to help him out. Shit, she even got him a password for the computer. Did Harold think this all just sprung out of nowhere—that magically, Derrick would show up and know exactly what to do? Did he have a plan at all?

Harold's blank eyes answered it all. Ericka took over the situation, as she always did.

"I think that's a great idea. Why don't you shadow me for a few days, to see behind the curtain? Then, perhaps, you can shadow Harold?"

"That sounds great," Harold said, eyes lowered and nodding. A beat of silence, two beats of silence—and if there were a clock in the room, certainly the ticking would have been like a gong reverberating between walls.

Derrick cut the silence, clearing his throat.

"Also, hey, I don't mean to be a bother, but I'm not sure when the right time is to bring this up. My computer isn't working. It's been spinning for about 20 minutes now, but it doesn't seem to be registering my user name or password."

Figures, Ericka thought to herself, brow furrowed. She tested it three times this morning, and it worked fine then. But, with the way fate worked in this office, it makes sense that as soon as it left her hands, something would go wrong and discredit her hard work. She tried to keep that disappointment from her face.

She then laughed, transparently fake, and waved her hand. “Don’t worry about it for now. I have a meeting in 10 minutes in the conference room, right there.” She pointed across the room, to a glass-walled conference room already filling with people. One person was sitting at the end of the table, at the head of it, wearing all black. Dennis. The man Derrick saw before.

Ericka wasn’t sure what she would do to show Derrick around, as she didn’t often touch the operational side. She also didn’t know what she was going to do about his computer, as their internal IT department was just one man named Stuart and he just left for a week-long vacation to the Poconos.

But she was going to figure it all out. She always did.

Chapter 10

"Now, to be clear, you don't have to understand or report on this meeting. You're just here to learn," Ericka said as she skimmed the papers on her desk until she found one—filled with handwritten notes. She closed her computer and grabbed a notebook.

"And don't worry about what people might say in there. It's definitely not a fun thing to deal with, but this kind of thing isn't the end of the world. We'll get it figured out. I'd like you to start seeing how we figure these things out, though."

"Definitely. Absolutely. I'm looking forward to it," Derrick said, though he wasn't sure if he meant it. It could be something to look forward to, or it could be completely over his head.

"You good?" Ericka said, really looking into his eyes.

"Oh yeah, I'm fine. Just absorbing it," Derrick said, unconvincingly. "It's just a lot to take in all at once, but that's a good thing. The first day is always the hardest, right?" He tried to sound more confident, but in all honesty, this was his first job in a physical office space, his first time acting professionally, and his first time given responsibilities that actually mattered.

"Okay, but you let me know if you're feeling overwhelmed, okay? We need you, but I also want to be sure you feel comfortable here. Things can go slower if you need them to," Ericka said. "We've never really had a new employee before, so this is new waters for us, too."

She had been a new employee, and she knew how it was to be a new employee learning this industry. There are the regular new-work hurdles, but there are also added hurdles in this. . . industry. There's a lot to wrap your head around, emotionally and logically.

And Derrick was picking up on this. Ever since he stepped into this building, things have seemed off. It was difficult to tell if it was because he was new and adjusting, or if there was something truly wrong with this facility—if there was something under the surface, trying to burst through the duct tape this entire department was held together by. Nobody seemed keen on telling him exactly what was happening. He had seen offices where everyone collaborated, and he saw offices where everyone seemed to not know what they were doing. This seemed to be the latter, but the stakes were much higher with a name like Death, Inc.

"If you need any paper to take any notes, you let me know. All you are expected to do is pay attention and learn. I want to let you know we're trying to construct an atmosphere of learning for you, so if you feel overwhelmed at any time, you let me know," Ericka said.

Derrick could tell that Ericka herself was overwhelmed. She was incredibly competent and had been professionally taking control here for some time. That part was clear. But underneath?

It seemed like there was an *oh, shit* hanging on the tip of her tongue every time something new came up, though she tried to hide that from appearing on her face.

She pushed a strand of hair behind her ear, looked at Derrick, and said, "Ready?"

The room was not a surprise. He could see it through the glass before he even entered it, but something about the air was stiller when he entered. Silence. Ericka sat on one side, the side opposite from the three others who were already sitting, but next to Dennis.

Now closer, he saw it was actually a charcoal grey turtleneck he was wearing under a black blazer. Mostly black.

Derrick sat next to Ericka, unsure if there was an unspoken courtesy in here that would explain for the silence.

"Good to see you well, Dennis," Ericka said as she opened her notebook.

"You too. Any idea how we're covering ourselves on this chickadee thing today, or are we just going in blind?" Dennis said, staring directly at the people who were setting up their presentation—what appeared to be a PowerPoint, using their new MacBook Pros to navigate it.

New MacBook Pros just to create fucking PowerPoints? Ericka thought. *How is that necessary?*

The three women huddled over the single computer screen—Susan, Denise, and Natalie—looked at Dennis, yet said nothing. Denise, in particular, was glowering, her eyes burning right below a carefully drawn brow. Immaculate. Precise. Uncomfortably so.

Ericka cleared her throat.

"I'm sure you've all noticed there is someone new in the room. We've hired a new marketing and PR rep to our team. Everyone, say hi to Derrick."

Nobody vocalized a greeting, but they did nod in his direction.

"We're happy to have you, Derrick. I think I saw you in the office next to mine. Let us know if you have any questions," Dennis said. Dennis, the one Derrick would probably not be working with all that much, Ericka had mentioned.

"It's a pleasure to meet you as well." He smiled at Dennis politely, then looked down the long conference desk—it appeared to be a long dining room table fit for 12 guests, give or take. Death, Inc. on one end, and New Beginnings on the other.

"We're here to talk about the soul-swapped chickadee," Susan said. She was a woman with a tidy blonde bob, mid-40s, and bright red lipstick. The one constantly in front of the coffee machine, a.k.a. Harold's archnemesis.

"*Alleged* soul-swapped chickadee," Dennis said, as if under his breath but loud enough for the entire table to hear it. He flipped to an empty page in his notebook.

"Excuse me?"

He sat erect, projected more, and looked down the conference desk. "We have yet to determine what exactly happened with this chickadee and whether anyone here is at fault. Or who. We are not going to take the fall for this completely with no basis."

"We have reason to believe that a chickadee received a human soul, rather than receiving a chickadee soul." Susan passed a note across the table:

"We found another one this morning. And our security footage picked up nothing other than the chickadee we believe to be leaving the note."

Dennis looked at Derrick and sighed. As if Derrick knew what was going on, as if he could relate already on his first day.

Derrick, however, was completely lost.

A chickadee with a human soul?

He didn't want to interrupt. If real, he knew there was too much to catch up on here, and wasn't sure where to start with questions. Or if now was the right time to ask questions. Or if he should even ask questions at all.

"I don't think it's unreasonable that we're opening a discussion on this. Do you think I'm being unreasonable? Denise?" Susan turned to her assistant, Denise—the one with the eerily symmetrically drawn brows one shade too dark for her light-brown hair.

"No, not unreasonable. We should really figure out what happened here," she said with less passion and a more matter-of-fact tone than Susan. As if she knew what she was saying was right, trying to sound logical above all else.

Susan's face was illuminated from below, casting an eerie blue-light glow as if she were telling a scary story around a campfire. "We've prepared a few slides to summarize where we're at with this, what we think we know but requires further investigation, and what our action plans are going forward to ensure this doesn't happen again."

Susan pulled up a slide that had a stock photo of a chickadee in the center, with the caption *chickadee with a human soul* below.

"As you can see here, we have outlined what we know now. Does anyone have any objections to the facts on this slide?"

It was clear this question wasn't for anyone on the other side of the table. It was clear this question was for Death, Inc. They sat in silence.

"Perfect. So we all agree that this human soul is currently in a chickadee body, thus explaining the notes left at our door for the past few months."

Dennis groaned.

Susan switched to the next slide—a plain white background with *How did a chickadee get a human soul?* in bolded Times New Roman font.

"This is what we do not know, based on our internal research. This is the main question we're trying to answer. Does this look correct to you?"

Again, this question was clearly directed toward Death, Inc.

What Derrick didn't know was this had been the third meeting that Dennis and Ericka had been to where they opened with these exact same slides. New Beginnings knew Death, Inc. didn't have any objections because they had already said, multiple times, in length, in person and in email, that they had no objections to these first two slides. To an infuriating degree.

"Perfect. Now, for the third slide. This is the conclusion we've come to, based on the information we have and the processes we know," Susan said, looking at the screen with a satisfied smirk.

Again, plain white background, with bolded Times New Roman font reading *Death, Inc. erroneously placed a human soul inside of a newborn chickadee.*

Dennis scoffed. "You realize how bullshit this is, correct? Where are your checks and balances?"

"We cannot catch everything, Dennis," Susan's assistant Denise said, thinly. "Inevitably, there will be some mistakes, but surely, we're not at fault for not catching yours. Where are yours?"

"Christ," Dennis said, leaning over the conference table and rubbing his temples. "This, again."

"We're not saying you're 100% at fault, Dennis. You share the blame. I hope you understand that it's not all on you," Susan said in a pseudo-saccharine voice, brows tilted upward.

"Oh, sorry. My coworkers take up the rest of the blame. The rest of the department is completely at fault, even though we're not going to address how this chickadee got this unwashed soul in the first place. Where are your checks and balances?"

"That is an issue for a different time—"

"Am I the only one who actually cares about this stuff?" Dennis scanned the room to find radio silence, other than Susan sighing, as if to say *here we go again with this soul thing.*

"What about you, Natalie?" Dennis then pointed to another woman sitting on that side of the table, black hair cut in a shoulder-length shag. By her retreating posture, she could not be a starker contrast to the blonde-bobbed Susan currently leading the meeting.

"What if one of your children was born with a maggot's soul? Would that hit home more—or would you still feel as apathetic?" Derrick wondered if he always spoke this theatrically, as if every line was rehearsed. Clean delivery, no stutters. Admirable.

"Dennis, this is not the purpose of today's meeting. If you want to address this very separate and not-as-pressing issue, you're going to have to set up a meeting that works for all of us later this week," Susan said with a sense of self-importance, an implied *look at this chump* smirk to the rest of her team. Denise smirked back, but Natalie remained silent, as if lost in the idea of her twin boys with maggot souls.

Ericka interjected. "We will investigate this on our side as well, to give a broader picture of what may have caused this." She looked at Dennis through her peripheral as she said this, checking his face to make sure he was in total agreement with what she was saying. "But at this time, I think it's safe to say that this PowerPoint presentation is not an accurate representation of what caused this incident."

Derrick nodded—not because he had any idea what was happening, but because he felt it was the right thing to do. To stand in solidarity with his team, as little as he knew about the situation he was getting himself into.

"That sounds great. Thank you, Ericka, for cooperating so we can get to the bottom of this issue," Susan said while looking daggers at Dennis. As if to say *thanks for nothing Dennis.* "Please review with your team this week, and we can meet with more of a prepared agenda next week. We hope to get this resolved as soon as we find the root. *Chop chop,* as they say."

Dennis left the table, closing the door before Susan could finish her sentence.

Another thing for my to-do list, Ericka thought.

Back in Ericka's office, Derrick was sitting in the chair across from her desk. So many questions hung on his tongue, but he wasn't sure which one would make the most sense to start with. It was like a *choose-your-own-adventure*—one question could lead him down one path of knowledge, while another could lead him down the other.

But what was the right question to ask?

"So, is this something that happens often, or is this an anomaly?" Derrick said. This seemed most important.

"I honestly can't think of a time this has happened since I started, but that's a surprise. We don't have the best system. To Dennis's point, that's why there should be more checks and balances. Christ . . ." she looked at Derrick as soon as *Christ* left her mouth. "I'm sorry for my French. You're not religious, are you?"

"No, I'm more of an agnostic."

"Good, that will make things easier all around. It's better to be separated from any spiritual or preconceived motions."

"I'm not entirely sure what you mean. I'm not entirely sure what I just listened in on, either, if you don't mind me saying. A bit hard for me to follow."

This was leading up to his next question—*what the fuck was that about?* Albeit this was a much more polite way to get to it.

"Of course. I'd imagine. Sometimes, I forget that this stuff isn't common knowledge. I've been working in it so long, you know? You forget what you knew before and what you learned along the way after that much time." Ericka wasn't addressing Derrick as she was talking with him. Instead, she was filing through papers on her desk trying to find something. "I'm sorry, I'm a bit all over the place. A crazy day over here."

"No problem—just let me know if there's anything I can do to help."

Ericka smiled. "That'll come, but for now, just watching and absorbing is the best thing you can do. Let's make it a goal to prep you to get that press release out by end of the week, okay?"

"I think what might actually help me is to see what we actually do here, versus listening in on more meetings. I hope that's not intrusive to say," Derrick said, intuiting that Ericka may need a bit of help to figure out what he needed and what would be helpful. *Sink or swim,* his grandfather's voice rang in his ear. He was not going to sink here.

"Of course. That totally makes sense. Here, let's go down there now. I have some work to do down there, anyway."

"The basement room?"

"Finally, let's get you some more info on that room. I'm sure that's been bugging you since you saw it, right?"

"That would be great," Derrick said. It had been bothering him, but he didn't want to look like a problematic employee. He was sure this stuff would become intuitive soon enough, and it was natural that nothing made sense in the beginning, right?

Ericka handed him some paper and a pen. "Here, something to take notes with. I have a feeling you're going to need it."

Chapter 11

"We use the stairs because sometimes the elevator doesn't go down all the way," Ericka explained as she opened the door to the stairwell. "It's usually reliable, but something about that basement floor . . . for some reason, it just doesn't like that basement floor."

"Odd," Derrick said without thought. He wasn't really listening—he was at capacity at this moment, kind of like how you feel after your aunt starts telling you how she *really* spent the to '70s after too many gin and tonics. He needed a breather and needed to turn his ears off until he was in that basement room.

"I'm sure it'll get fixed eventually, but I've gotten stuck in that thing three times—and that's more than I ever want to get stuck in anything, you know?"

"Definitely," Derrick said, twirling the pen between his fingers. A nervous habit. A way to focus his energy.

"I know it's a lot to process right now, but hopefully this will give you some context," Ericka said as she descended the stairs ahead of him, rather than hanging behind to walk with him. She was filling empty space with empty words. She didn't like that, but she didn't want to acknowledge it. Instead, she walked ahead.

At the first flight of stairs, both were wondering if the other would say something.

At the second flight, both were wondering if they should say something.

At the third, both thought that maybe they should wait to speak until they got into the room, where they would go over procedures.

At the fourth, Ericka sneezed. Derrick said, "Bless you."

At the fifth, Ericka wondered why there was nobody else in the stairwell. Usually she passed at least one person.

This thought continued to the sixth flight down.

At the seventh flight, Derrick wondered if it was his responsibility as the new guy to break the ice, if he was the one who should be asking questions.

Finally, the eighth flight. Both let out an internal sigh of relief.

Stairwells are a great place to walk if you're all alone, where you're able to simply think while walking toward your destination. But when you're walking with someone else, with someone you don't know well, it can be a literal hell.

Ericka punched in the door code and said, "It gets easier. My thighs are definitely more defined than some of my friends' thighs, that's for sure." Too much information to tell her new coworker, someone she'd be supervising? Maybe. She moved past it.

"I know Harold already showed you this room, but it probably seemed like a bit of a blur. I think this will be helpful to know our process, though, after the meeting we just had." Ericka looked at the machine, silent. "We can't work on any active cases now, but I can show you how it would go, should there be one."

"Sounds great," Derrick said. He followed Ericka, noting not to get too close or too far. This room felt like the stairwell, but at least they had something to talk about. now. At least it wasn't just step after step of silence.

"This is the room where we process the souls," Ericka said plainly, as if she were explaining what she had for breakfast that morning.

Derrick froze. "Excuse me?"

"I'm sure that's a lot to take in. I'm sorry. It's been a while since I've learned this. It just seems so common to me now."

Derrick was nervous, trying to keep his distance while following Ericka toward the first machine, the one that spits out the receipt paper that Harold referenced. The one that somehow signified Harvey Nelson. Derrick didn't want to walk too close, but he also wanted to see what Ericka was referencing. A careful balance.

"This is where we get notified of the soul that is departing a body. This is technically called a Mortal Signifying Number, or MSN, meaning a number assigned to a soul as soon as it's given a body to live within," Ericka said.

"And how does that happen, exactly?"

"It spits out the machine."

"Apologies, I mean before it spits out the machine."

"A person dies."

"But how do we know a person dies?"

"Dennis takes care of that. We're not privy to his processes."

Derrick was dumbfounded. "I'm not understanding. This looks like you're killing people to me. This looks like a really elaborate way to kill people."

There was a silence in the room, a drip of water somewhere off in the corner that echoed between the brick foundation walls, painted white probably 20 years ago by the looks of their wear.

Another drip, before Ericka responded.

"Perhaps if you see the entire process, that will give you a better idea of what we do," she continued, apprehensively. As if dipping her bare toe into a stream she knew would be cold.

"Okay," Derrick said, unperturbed.

"This *is* a lot to process, which is exactly why we need you here. To make things more . . . palatable, should we ever need to address the press. You will be helping us a lot by better understanding and explaining in a way I don't think we can."

Derrick wasn't sure what to say, so he said nothing.

"Well, let's get started." Ericka turned back to the first machine Harold ripped the register tape from, resting her hand on it as she said, "As I mentioned before, this is where we receive a Mortal Signifying Number, or MSN. We are notified that an MSN is coming in by email as it is being printed. That is an automatic process, so you do not have to worry about that. I'll show you what one looks like once it comes in."

"What is a Mortal Signifying Number?"

"An MSN tells us how many times a soul has been used in a mortal being, along with its unique identifying number. These two numbers together create the MSN. New Beginnings has files that list which MSN is attached to which person, which is transferred as citizens move in and out of town—as long as they change their address, of course, or register their move, which you should always do because it makes our job so, so much easier," Ericka said. "But I'm deviating. The MSN. That makes sense now?"

"I think so. So it's basically our soul's identifying number?"

"Your soul's unique identifying number, as well as what iteration it's on, correct. Basically, it's the identifying number plus an iteration stamp. And this list is compiled by the Birthing Department—sorry, New Beginnings. As soon as someone is born and a soul is recycled, they create a new MSN for the new bundle of joy."

"This makes sense," Derrick said. Using his hand as a writing pad, he scribbled "MSN-soul ID-Mortal Signifying Number-soul's identifying number-iteration number-Birthing Department." The creases in his hand made the writing difficult to read. He remembered the paper in his pocket after he accidentally smudged the ink.

"Wait, recycled? Are souls recycled?" Derrick asked.

"I think that will make sense soon, if you don't mind. As soon as you see the whole picture."

Ericka picked up the first folder and pulled out a piece of paper. On the paper, three columns. Each of the three columns contained a number and a name.

"This is a list of active souls in our town. Those crossed out are those who are unfortunately no longer with us." She paused as she flipped the page to the end. "This is updated every year, but when there are births, we add them manually to the last page. This list ties an MSN to the human it inhabits."

Derrick continued to write information down: "Folder 1 MSN + human name New Beginnings added manually with each birth." Now, he was writing on the paper Ericka had given him, using his palm as a mini desk. His pen went through the paper and lightly stabbed his palm.

Ericka put the packet of paper back into the folder and picked up the next folder, to its right. She took out another packet. Similar length.

"This list matches a person's name to the Soul Signifying Number, its core number. This is the number without its iteration, its true identifier. We call this an SSN. When there is a problem with a soul that can be traced through several MSNs, we reference it by its SSN and retire it." Ericka cleared her throat.

Derrick looked at her, blankly.

Ericka continued. "So, if you look here, you'll see a person's name next to a slightly shorter number. That slightly shorter number is the SSN. This SSN is what we need to enter into this box, here."

Derrick hurried to write down the folder stuff, "Folder 2 SSN slightly shorter + name write down SSN" before Ericka continued to explain what the second box was. He knew none of these notes would make sense, but he hoped they would at least help him connect the dots later.

"You'll need to enter the SSN in by typing it in here." She put her hand on top of the machine with the faded bulldog sticker on its side. Derrick looked closer at it—simply an old 1960s-style keyboard, like a Selectric, attached to a 2-foot square cube with a receipt printer on the top.

"Is there a screen that shows which numbers have been typed, or—"

"There should be, right? But no, there's no way to tell until you've printed it out. I usually double check before I even begin to type. That is important. Always make sure you're writing these numbers down, because if you screw up these numbers, well . . . that could screw up someone's life, you know?"

"Have there been any instances of that? What would that look like?"

"Not in my career, no, so I can't say for certain what that would look like exactly. It wouldn't be excellent though, I'm guessing."

As Ericka made her way to the third folder, Derrick wrote more down: "Box 2 no screen SSN check double check deadly if not." He was hoping that he'd remember what these notes meant by adding what they were talking about around this. Like a scent reminding you of a specific memory, he hoped these details would help to trigger his memory so he would remember more.

"Oh, I almost forgot," Ericka said as she dropped the third folder and went to the fourth. She opened it and turned to him—the first time she was really addressing him since they came into this room. "This is most important step, but one that we have to keep a bit on the down low. You will *always* have to check the numbers to make sure none of these numbers are being passed on. Think of it like a suppression list."

"A what?"

"A list of people we can't let die. Does this make sense?"

"So we're purposely keeping them alive, no matter what?"

"Precisely."

Ericka handed him the list. There were several names on there. Most notably on the top, Dave Grohl.

"This is a list of all the people we cannot kill, for one reason or another. We keep a master list of those. You never know if someone will be traveling at their time of death, meaning their death would be processed elsewhere. Better to be safe."

Derrick looked through the names to see if there were any he knew. Dave Grohl and Henry Rollins were two that stood out the most. Kathleen Hanna, too. Cordozar Calvin Broadus, Jr. with the annotation "Snoop Dogg" written in pen below. Frank Huguelet, with the annotation "Ric Savage" written in pen below. Amy Winehouse was notably crossed out. Chris Farley was notably crossed out.

But there was one he didn't expect.

“Isn’t this the front desk girl?” Derrick pointed to Anissa’s name. He recognized it from the distribution list Ericka had given him earlier that day.

She didn’t respond, only nodded.

“I need to emphasize how important it is that we do not talk about this list. This list stays between you, me, and Harold. Dennis cannot know about this list. *Especially* Dennis.” Ericka brushed her hair behind her ear, as if she knew she was asking a lot of him, but she also knew she needed it. “This list is a department secret, but it is sacred. Please always reference this list, should you ever find yourself in this room processing souls while you work here.”

“Understood,” Derrick said quietly.

“Please don’t write that in your notes. I’d rather not have any evidence I told you of this.” Ericka took the paper from Derrick and looked through it once more before putting it back in the folder. She put the folder under the table, on top of a box.

“Always be sure to put it away as well. We cannot let this folder be found.”

“But why is the secretary on this list? It looks like she’s in a lot of pain. Does that have anything to do with the list?”

“There are some questions I cannot answer for you, unfortunately. Not because I’m not allowed, but because I truly don’t know. I’m only told that we cannot kill anyone on that list, and I’ve stuck with that. But, as I mentioned, she cannot know. Nobody can know. This is our secret, along with Harold’s.”

“Understood,” Derrick said, stopping himself from taking notes at the last minute. He had one more question, but visibly decided to restrain it. Ericka smiled at his restraint and nodded.

“Thank you. Now, finally, the last part.” Ericka lifted the third folder, significantly thinner than the last. In it was the piece of paper Harold said “this is where you put all of the numbers” or something akin to that.

Ericka said, “This is where you document the SSN of the recently deceased, to be recycled by New Beginnings. They take this paper and rip the receipts off once they’ve used them.

All you do is staple that receipt onto this paper, and there you have it. Put it back in the folder, then put it in the outbox."

Derrick didn't have any more room on his paper, so he repeated this information in his head. If he repeated it enough in his head, he reasoned, he'd be able to write it down once he got upstairs.

"Any questions?"

Derrick had so, so many questions, but he didn't think any of them would be productive at the time.

"I think I understand the basics for now, but I'm sure I'll have questions as soon as I dive in."

"Of course. It's probably time for lunch anyway, if you want to take an hour to decompress. I know we've thrown a lot at you."

Derrick took a full lunch hour. He took it in his office looking through his notes. The notes that, now, made no sense, as he assumed they wouldn't.

MSN-soul ID-Mortal Signifying Number-soul's identifying number + iteration number-Birthing Department.

What? he said under his breath as he reviewed this. His own notes looked like wingdings in retrospect.

Folder 1 MSN + human name New Beginnings added manually with each birth. His brow furrowed as he reread this note.

Folder 2 SSN slightly shorter + name write down SSN

Box 2 no screen SSN check double check deadly if not

Below that, he wrote *double check* again, hoping he'd be able to remember this meant Folder 4.

Below that, he wrote *staple receipt paper outbox.*

He looked at his notes again.

No sense. None of this made any sense.

Maybe it would be better to draw the room, so he could visualize it.

Still no sense.

But partly because he could not stop thinking about what lay in Folder 4. The one he wasn't supposed to talk about. The one he couldn't even write about. The folder he saw the contents of, but could not speak on.

Why the fuck would a list like that exist? Derrick made a mental note to ask Ericka more on this later.

He opened his laptop, still spinning.

He ate his lunch alone in his office—a peanut butter sandwich with a side of carrots. He crunched every carrot as quietly as he could—he didn't want to be a burden. Everyone else seemed busy, and the walls were paper thin.

But why was Anissa's name on there? Alongside Dave Grohl, Henry Rollins, Kathleen Hanna, Snoop, Ric Savage. Why was Anissa included?

Chapter 12

Anissa's ribs hurt. Badly. They do tell you not to move when you have bruised ribs. They don't tell you that you can't sit up. Or maybe they do?

Maybe she just chose to ignore that part.

Oh. They definitely tell you that, she realized as she scrolled through Webline Plus's article "Bruised Rib Care" on her iPhone. *Not supposed to be sitting. Supposed to be laying down.*

They had never hurt this bad, though. She had resumed a relatively normal life before, when she had bruised her ribs previously, but now?

Now it seemed unbearable. Perhaps she had broken them.

Or perhaps there was so much damage done to them at this point that this pain would just continue to get worse, the more things like this happened.

She could tell it wasn't internal damage. The pain was located in her ribs, and didn't go deeper than that. She knew deeper pain. This was definitely a bone pain. A sharp pain. It stabbed her every time she moved, even slightly. Breathing wasn't entirely painful until she thought about it. Only when she thought about it did she notice the dull, monotonous throb that was now her baseline.

She continued to search "bruised or fractured ribs" and "what to do with fractured ribs" and "working with fractured ribs" and "working with bruised ribs" and "fractured ribs can't get off duty" and "mitigate pain fractured ribs" when a text from Gary appeared on her screen.

Gary: "Hey Niss—going to be late tonight. We have to pick up my mom from the airport. Be there around 7?"

Anissa was now reliant on her friends, her roommates, to help her to and from work. This was partly because her car was totaled, but partly because she was too injured to drive.

Fuck, she thought, wondering what there was to do for two hours. Her phone was starting to die. There was an Applebee's next door. That's a good way to make some friends she didn't want to, and while she could normally fend for herself, she was in no mood to shoo anyone away tonight or to deny a free Long Island, as she knew she should.

Should I ask Derrick? she thought. Admittedly, this nice gesture would be done for the wrong reasons. Not the *wrong* reasons, but not as wholly selfless, as they seemed on their face.

Perhaps no good deed is wholly selfless. Perhaps no selfish deed is wholly selfish.

"Okay, np" she replied, then continued to look for bruised rib remedies.

***

Derrick was dreading going to the lobby. He had waited in his office for this very reason. He didn't know if he could face Anissa at the front desk, knowing what he knew. That she was on the list.

What does that even mean? Derrick thought. He wasn't certain. He had no idea what any of it meant. But talking with her, knowing this? He knew he'd have to, eventually. It's not like he could just jump out of the window and land in his Honda.

But he could stall. Hope she wouldn't be there anymore. Hope she went home early. He couldn't imagine that there would be any secretarial needs past 4:30 pm. Perhaps she went home early. He waited in his office until 5:30 pm, to be sure.

"What are you doing in there?" Ericka said as she passed his open door, doing a double take.

"Oh, nothing. Just getting settled," Derrick said to Ericka as she was on her way out.

"You don't need anything from me, do you? Just want to be sure I'm not leaving you high and dry."

"Nope, not high and dry. I'm low and wet over here," he said, followed by an immediate stab of embarrassment to his chest. *Why do I always go one step too far? Why do I say these things?* The jokes always sounded way funnier in his head, but whenever they came out of his mouth, deadpan. Uncomfortable.

"Well, that sounds like something you should keep to yourself," Ericka said jokingly. "Have a nice night, though! Don't stay too late. See you tomorrow."

The good news is Derrick got his computer working again. *Finally.* Just as he was about to take it into Harold's office, or Ericka's office, or someone's office, the wheel arbitrarily stopped spinning.

Only six hours after it started, give or take.

It was no dramatic sort of accomplishment. It seemed like a technological whim, something that just happened when the mainframe deemed it "the correct time to start up."

The Lenovo desktop was blank. His email, Outlook, was already downloaded, his credentials already entered. All he had to do was log in.

There were a few emails in his inbox already, but nothing of importance. A very sweet email from Ericka welcoming him, with attachments of the documents she already gave him. An email from Harold with a request marked *urgent*, but it didn't seem urgent.

He searched "how to avoid someone who is in the same room as you" and "how to have uncomfortable conversations" and the like.

All of the articles seemed to assume that he was breaking up with someone. None seemed to give any legitimate advice on what he was dealing with now.

He searched once more: "how to effectively avoid someone."

No luck.

He looked at the clock. *5:35 pm*. Perhaps she was already gone for the day, and it wouldn't even be an issue. Perhaps he could just hurry out.

Sure. He'd do that. He wasn't about to spend his night in the office. He needed to get home at some point. He had to leave the office eventually.

But as soon as he entered the lobby, he heard a voice behind him.

"Hey! I was wondering when you'd be down." Anissa said from her desk. "I'm here late. Want to go to Applebee's?"

Derrick paused. This was exactly the opposite of what he was trying to do. He was trying to never talk with her again, to make sure the secret would never get out. To make sure he wouldn't completely blow it. He fumbled with his words, trying to decide what would be the least conspicuous negative response, given his circumstances.

"Sure," he said.

Shit, he thought.

That's not what he meant to say. A curse—naturally, a people pleaser.

"You don't have to if you don't want to. I can go myself. It's no big deal if you have plans tonight, or something. I was just wondering, seeing as you're new here, and all."

Well, he couldn't say no, now. He had to double down on his accidental response.

"No, I think that'd be fun! It would be good to get to know people in the office," Derrick said, unnaturally quick.

"Okay! Okay, cool. Sounds great!" She started to pack her things. "You don't mind driving, do you? It's just I hurt my ribs, and it's a bit difficult to drive."

"Are you okay?" Derrick noticed as she grimaced when she stood up.

"Oh, this? I was in an accident, but it's totally cool. I've got a bit of a curse on me, you know? Makes me tough, but wow, does it hurt."

Derrick flinched—visibly trying to keep the secret in.

"I would say I can relate, but—"

"Totally fine. I shouldn't have said anything. Do you mind giving me a lift? I know it's right there, but might be easier."

"Of course. No problem at all. I can drive us there."

"To be clear, this isn't a date. I just thought. . ."

Derrick hadn't thought of it that way—but, on top of being incredibly nervous about exposing the folder, now there was this looming over their conversations.

"Oh, no. Just friends. Just getting to know each other. I totally agree."

"No dating in the workplace," Anissa said shaking her finger, mocking.

They drove to Applebee's with Derrick's *Appetite for Destruction* playing louder than he remembered setting the volume this morning. This morning might as well have been 10 days ago.

He didn't turn it down. He probably should have, but that would have meant they had to talk. So he kept it playing at full volume. She didn't say anything—just looked out the window for the two-minute drive until they got there.

Chapter 13

Applebee's is always so aggressively lit, while still being incredibly dim. A miracle. There are lights everywhere, but if you're not under a light or your overhead light is out, you're kind of shit-out-of-luck on reading the menu.

I don't think they expect you to read the menu. I think they just assume you're a regular, even if it's your first time. They assume you're a regular at some Applebee's, somewhere—that you are, in some way, shape, or form a part of the Applebee's Extended Universe.

"I don't think I've been to an Applebee's in at least five years," Anissa said as they were being seated by a woman who didn't even ask them how many would be at their table. She just saw them as soon as they walked through the door and flagged them to follow her, in one slick hand motion.

"Same," Derrick said. His hands were shoved nervously in his hoodie pockets.

Don't give this away, Derrick. You can't tell her about the folder. You must keep this a secret. Don't even get close to it. His head psyched him up for the conversation where he would not reveal anything he learned at work today, or most importantly, anything that affected her.

He started to rehearse things to talk about in his head, things that might be smooth conversations that would in no way breach what he saw at work that day. Favorite vacation spots. Childhood memories. Hobbies. Are there any good parks in the area? And so on. Anything to avoid spouting out that her name was on the list. What the list was. What he did. Any of it.

"Livin' on a Prayer" played quietly, muffled, as if it was playing from a cell phone speaker lodged somewhere in the popcorn ceiling.

Anissa walked a bit slower behind while holding her side, still trying to keep up. She was trying to keep her torso still as she walked. You never realize how much your body moves until you hurt a vital part of its movement.

Ribs. The worst thing to injure.

Derrick slid into the booth as the hostess waited with two menus in hand. A solid *3, 2, 1* occurred before Anissa slid into the booth as well, carefully. Careful not to move her ribs too much, if that was possible. It didn't seem successful, based on her wince.

Anissa knew that, if she had seen a doctor, they'd be pissed at her right now. She moved past it.

"Thanks for waiting. Sorry about that," she said, attempting to address her lag, but coming up short.

"No, no worries. You're fine," Derrick said as the hostess slid their menus in front of them. Where a waitress would usually say "Thank you for coming to Applebee's!" or list the specials, she instead sighed and walked away.

But she wasn't in a hurry. She walked slowly, silently returning to her post in the front. The rest of the restaurant was empty. She pulled out her phone from underneath the hostess table and hunched over, a screen glow creating a silhouette of arched shoulders. Muffled, they could hear what we can only assume to be TikTok, a rapid succession of dissonant sounds, oscillating between songs and unsolicited inspirational monologues.

"So, first day, huh? That's exciting," Anissa said as she scanned the menu. Their eyes met as she looked over the edge of the laminated drink menu. Her eyes smiled. His looked down.

"Yeah, I guess," Derrick cleared his throat. "I mean, not that exciting. Not too exciting. Not terribly exciting," Derrick said, wondering if he was too heavy on the disinterest. "I mean, I like it, don't get me wrong, but it's not like we're solving world hunger or anything up there. It's not like I don't like the job, it's just that there's nothing interesting to talk about with it."

If she could've, she would've leaned forward to show she cared. Instead, she let her eyes talk—one eyebrow raised to show she was listening and engaged as much as she could before saying, "Did something happen today? Do you need to talk?"

That was the exact opposite of what Derrick wanted to do.

With Derrick, keeping a secret was like bringing a balloon into a room filled with angry bees. Not only would that balloon pop, most certainly, but it was probably going to be a painful process leading up it.

"No, nothing happened—just my first day. You know how that is. First-day jitters. Sorry if I seem nervous. It's because it's my first day," Derrick said in one long, uninterrupted string of excuses.

As we all do in uncomfortable situations, we usually blame ourselves. Anissa was across the booth blaming herself. Surely, she had done something to cause this. Perhaps she made him feel awkward by asking him to come out in the first place. Perhaps it was something she said early on. Perhaps she was asking too many questions, as she knew she often did when she was getting to know someone. She retreated into her head, trying to think of a way to fix this social break.

Anissa went with, "I get that."

Derrick's shoulders relaxed a bit. Not completely, but a bit.

She continued, "Did you know this is only my third week? They called me out of the blue to come in for an interview, hadn't even submitted an application. I thought *what the heck*, you know? They're hiring like crazy right now. Good time to be with them, I guess."

Curious, Derrick thought. He wondered who had called Anissa and desperately fought the urge to ask. He didn't want to dive into it.

"Yeah, when they need people they need people," Derrick said, but he wasn't exactly sure what he meant by that.

"So, what did they hire you for?" Anissa asked.

"Marketing or PR," Derrick said as the hostess arrived with two glasses of water. She lifted up two straws as if to say "Straws?" They both shook their heads.

"I never understood straws. It seems like such an unnecessary middleman," Anissa said as soon as the hostess left.

"They're wasteful," Derrick said.

"That, too." Anissa took a sip of water and was thankful to see the waitress on her way back to take their order.

Anissa got the special salad, but she couldn't remember what was on it. Derrick got ribs. He'd had them before at a few locations, and they weren't bad. He'd had some difficulties with one Applebee's in his past, so he avoided everything outside of ribs and fries, out of remembrance and precaution.

"So, marketing. PR? That seems interesting. I didn't know they did any marketing up there, but I guess I have no idea what they do up there, anyway. What is it, Death, Inc.? Sounds rad. How did you find it?"

"Craigslist," Derrick said.

"Oh, wow, Craigslist. I haven't used that in ages."

"It's useful. Got a bookshelf off it last week," Derrick said, trying to steer the conversation away from work, but with limited options. "The church down the street from my house was just giving them away. It's scratched to hell, but it does have a nice look to it, if you put something on top of it." He wished he had more to say. His arm grew tired from forcing the metaphorical rudder against this conversational current.

"Do you ever refab furniture? I have some small pieces, these wooden boxes from my grandma, that I'd love to honor in some way." *Finally,* Anissa thought. She found something more comfortable to talk about. Less capitalism-is-the-devil focused—at least, not on its face. She'd pay him, obviously, if he did any work for her, but she was more asking to get him talking about something he liked.

"I'm not excellent at it but . . ."

Their conversation continued from there, but with no direction. While still not completely natural, they got to know each other's quirks on the surface and were able to better assess as they continued to talk. Then eat. Then talk over a drink—the bar insisted they take the happy hour special that ended an hour ago, on the house.

“Dang, we should go here more often,” Anissa said as she took a sip of a Long Island, thankful she didn’t have to drive as soon as she smelled it.

“I haven’t been to an Applebee’s in ages,” Derrick said again. “But this was fun! Thank you for getting me out!”

Anissa smiled. “We should make this a regular thing. How about every Monday, to start off the week? I don’t really hang out with anyone from work, and it’d be fun to have a friend there. If you don’t mind.”

Derrick paused for a second, and lifted his pint glass for a sip of some lager he ordered blindly. There was no way he could keep this secret if they met every Monday for drinks. There was no way he wouldn’t crack eventually, even if it wasn’t the whole secret he was keeping. In his rational mind, he knew that agreeing to this would be a death sentence.

But now? Though he had only one beer, he was riding the high of a good conversation that he was sure would tank and destroy his brand-new career. This dinner ending without him completely blowing all of Death Inc’s secrets right away? He may as well have had 10 beers with how relaxed he felt.

“That sounds awesome. Yeah, I’m down,” Derrick said.

Later that night, as he lay in bed trying to sleep, his stomach turned. Delayed regret. What had he done?

Chapter 14

"Hey, Derrick!" Anissa said as soon as he got in the next day. "Get home alright last night?"

He paused and tried to be natural, wondering if it would always be like this. If she could pick up on it. How could he continue this?

"Hey! Good morning," Derrick said as he rushed past her. "Sorry, I'm running late—I've got a thing."

"Wouldn't want to be late on your second day!" Anissa turned to shout this as he got in the elevator, which hurt her side. She had slept on it funnily the night before, despite Gary and Stephanie making sure she was surrounded by pillows to limit her motion at least the one time she could sit still.

You really should be staying at home, they said. She wondered if they were right, as she felt her side throbbing again.

"Good morning, Dennis!" Anissa said as cheerfully as she could through a grimace.

"Good morning, Anissa. Sorry, I can't talk," Dennis said as he ran to catch Derrick's elevator.

"So, I see you've met Anissa," Dennis said as soon as the doors closed. "Between you and me, I'm not sure if that's a good idea."

Derrick paused, wondering his angle. Dennis wasn't supposed to know about the folder, but did he anyway? He seemed to have that air to him—of just knowing things naturally, without anyone telling him.

"She invited me to dinner, but it's just as work friends. Nothing more serious than that," Derrick assured.

Dennis nodded. "Well, that's good. I'm glad to hear that. That's better than I thought." He ran his hands through his hair. "This job isn't easy, you know? Knowing who is going to die soon."

Derrick stood at one of the elevator corners, surprised.

"Don't mention to anyone I told you that, but I figured you should know." A pause for five beats, then the doors opened abruptly. Dennis stepped out and continued. "Have a good day, Derrick. Let me know if you need anything."

Derrick stood in the elevator for a minute, uncertain how to process that information. There's no way Anissa should get hurt again in her condition. Perhaps her ribs would get worse, or perhaps she would fall because her injury and hurt herself more.

"Hey Derrick, are you going to join us?" Ericka said as she looked into the elevator.

Derrick jolted from his trance and shook his head. "Sorry—I got lost in a thought," he said as he exited the elevator, toward his office.

"That was rude of me, sorry. I mean to say hello, and welcome back to your second day," Ericka said as she walked with Derrick. "I've left some things on your desk for you to review, some things that I think might help you out. No action items, just knowledge." In her hand was a mug of coffee filled exactly to the brim. She carried the cup from the top, to ensure it maintained equilibrium, to ensure she minimized spill risk by creating a stable center of gravity.

"Thanks! I'll take a look at those. Is there anything else you need from me?" He was still uncertain what his job would be exactly, so he planned on asking this question every morning until he got a full answer.

"We have a meeting at 10:00 am, but other than that, nothing but learning." Ericka realized how fake her voice sounded, how motherly. This kid was technically in her generation, but there's so much development that happens through your 20s. She forgot how innocent she used to be five years ago. How much had happened since then?

"Awesome, thanks," Derrick said, noting how kind Ericka was despite the audible chaos coming from behind a shut door. Harold's office.

What it was, Derrick couldn't make out. He was hoping he'd be able to hear better from his office, maybe, where there was less ambient noise.

"It's just not right!" was all Derrick could make out, said with a staccato end to each word. As if there were an exclamation point at the end of each word.

On Derrick's desk were two pieces of paper. One was a slide from the previous day's presentation, showing the picture of a chickadee with the caption *Chickadee with a human soul* below. The second note was a dense, 10pt font, filled with notes from their previous meetings.

The bastards, Derrick could safely assume he could say. He could feel the animosity in the tone of the meeting notes. The "we know this is overkill, but we have to" tone resonated from every sentence. Ericka left.

In Ericka's handwriting on a Post-it note on the top of the pile, she wrote, "Not necessary for you to know backward and forward, but thought some context might help. Happy Day 2 ☺."

Derrick opened his computer and saw the email from Harold again. He opened it, but inside the email was a series of attachments. No notes.

There were only news articles that Harold wanted him to address at some point, but Harold put no effort into explaining that within the email. Derrick replied, "Hi Harold, what would you like me to do with these? Are these for context, or are these action items?" He decided to say "Happy Tuesday" before signing his name. Friendlier.

Derrick would have stopped by his office, had he not been in the middle of yelling. Still yelling.

"That's not what it said on the warranty!" Harold shouted again. *Was this work-related?* he wondered. Not that it mattered. Not that Derrick was any sort of judge. He could not judge competence at this point. He only had his first impressions, which he was trying to temper.

This is none of my business, Derrick said under his breath. He had to focus. He could not jeopardize this job by getting judgmental.

He skimmed a few of the newspaper articles Harold had attached. Some were from 20 years ago, photocopied from their physical originals and saved onto his computer, he assumed. Or however there was record of things happening.

These may actually be helpful—may be able to tell what Death, Inc. is really doing, outside of the soul intake process, if that's what you'd call it, that he saw the day before (which still didn't make much sense).

From May 1987, the *Schuester Chronicles* (what the newspaper used to be called, before people began to say it sounded too folklore-ish): "Folder containing list of recently deceased Schuster citizens was found in a McDonald's parking lot on Saturday, with Death, Inc. letterhead on the top. We tried to reach Death, Inc. for comment, yet got nothing. We will continue to investigate and will report once we know more."

From 1989: "Secretary from Death, Inc. tells it all in this gripping account of death, life, power, struggle, love, and everything else you can think of." Derrick looked around this office and wondered where this journalist was getting all that excitement from this department. Perhaps things were different back then.

From 1992: "Death, Inc. moves into the bigger warehouse on the south side of town—you know, where the old Polish sausage company used to be." Ah, that would explain it. They used to be somewhere else. "We are still investigating the fire that inexplicably burned down the previous Death, Inc. headquarters, shared by their partners Life Birth Inc (they tell us this is a working name, as they continue to rebrand their image)." Derrick wrote down *ask about the fire.* This seemed important.

From 1996: "A Death, Inc. employee was found dead under mysterious circumstances."

How had Derrick never heard of these stories before? The first time he had heard of Death, Inc. was from the Craigslist ad he answered? He knew where the quarry was that was a town secret. He knew that the only gas station in town used to be a mortuary, and that they used the gurneys for food prep, now. He thought he knew everything about this town.

How did this escape his radar?

Google. Maybe Google will be able to tell him.

But when he tried to Google Death, Inc., again, nothing. He found only a few things that were most certainly not related: a popular video game streaming on Steam, a coffee company, and a strange blog run by someone who appeared to think they were a zombie, with little show of whether this was fictionalized or if the author legitimately thought they were the living dead. So, so, so many bands, including one metal band that didn't look too bad from Scranton, Pennsylvania.

Nothing tied to this company seemed to be popping up.

"Hi, Derrick. Is there anything I can help you with? Have you had a chance to read your notes?" In the time Derrick was reading the first blog post from the blog titled Death, Inc., Ericka managed to grab him a coffee and set it on his desk without him noticing.

He jumped, closed his computer halfway, then said, "Oh, God! Oh, I'm sorry, I didn't see you there—you scared me a bit."

"I'm so sorry—I didn't realize you were so focused," Ericka said, wondering what he was so interested in, but pushing it aside in her mind. They had thrown a lot at him, so even if he was surfing Reddit, she couldn't blame him. He probably deserved a mental break.

"Apologies. Thank you for the coffee. Nothing too important, just reading over some things Harold sent me before I dive back into these notes," Derrick said.

"Oh?" Ericka didn't mean to sound annoyed, but she didn't realize Harold would be sending him anything yet. That hadn't been what they agreed on. They agreed they'd guide him toward getting the press release done through conversation, through giving him the information that he needed verbally and to be there as mentors as he figured it out. Sending an email was certainly not effective mentorship, at least not in Ericka's mind.

"I'm curious—what did he send you?" Ericka asked, sitting down in a chair across from Derrick's desk.

"Just some news articles to look over. Nothing too crazy."

“Do you mind forwarding that to me as well? I’m wondering if I can provide some context surrounding that. I’d imagine you’re feeling a bit overwhelmed as it is, so if there’s any way I can help—”

“No problem. I can forward them to you.” Derrick opened his computer and sent them on.

Ericka took a sip of her coffee. “Well, I don’t think I have anything else for you until 10:00 am—unless you have questions. Let me know if you need anything. I’ll be in my office.”

Ericka opened the email in her office, saw the attachments, and immediately got a headache.

Not that it was a disaster. It was just embarrassing, and a lot she’d have to explain. Eventually. Soon. Or at least add context for this poor, poor kid who has just been thrown in the deep end since yesterday.

Chapter 15

Ericka sat across the conference table from Harold, Dennis, and Derrick. While she didn't expect Derrick to be prepared, he was the one who looked most prepared—in that he was the only one to actually look mentally present. Dennis was picking at a corner of the table, where the laminate was peeling up, and Harold was staring in the distance, his mind elsewhere.

Ericka cleared her throat, trying to gain control of the room that was already two-thirds lost. "We're here to talk about the chickadee, again," Ericka said. "Did you guys bring your slides? I'm hoping we can just take notes on that, and that will be sufficient."

"I mean, I think it's pretty cut and dry, right?" Dennis said. It was clear he had just printed the slides out right before this meeting. The ink slightly smeared at any touch. That, and Ericka saw him do it. He smiled and waved as he printed out materials that she had prepared all night for, or so it felt.

She had thought about it all night, pondered over a mug of tea and tried to make sense of it as she dozed off on her floral-patterned loveseat.

At least they trusted her enough to let her completely take the wheel, she reasoned. She just wished they put forth some effort. Any.

Harold was now buried in his phone set on the table, scrolling clumsily with his pointer finger. "I didn't have time to print them out, but I have it pulled up on my cellular device," he said. He had recently gotten a cell phone, as the office building was starting to remove all landlines from the facility. He was currently at the *I can use this for everything and I am its master* phase of the technological learning curve, but didn't fully understand what he was doing or how to do it effectively.

"Don't worry—I printed out an extra set for you." Ericka slid the packet across the table until it landed in front of him. He paused, then furrowed his brow as he picked it up.

"So, this chickadee thing seems to have created quite a stir," Harold said.

"For unnecessary reasons. It's not our fault. Plain and simple. We did nothing wrong," Dennis said, eyes unfocused but directed downward. "I can provide the proof, if necessary, but why should we for these power vultures? They just want to be right."

Harold nodded. "He does have a point. Ericka, have we thought about just not telling the Birthing Department—"

"New Beginnings," she corrected him.

"Have you thought about telling the Birthing Department that it's not our responsibility to give them a reason, and that they should continue their investigation internally?"

"Harold, with all due respect—"

"I know it will be difficult, but this will be a great learning opportunity for you. Great professional leadership development." Harold looked at Derrick, wondering if he should have Derrick break the news as well. He wore the sudden realization on his face with an eyebrow raise, then a visible pause for thought.

Derrick saw it, but tried to avoid eye contact. He absorbed himself into the slides, looking at the front and then the page of notes Ericka had created for him.

"There was a mix-up at the soul exchange level, and we are trying to investigate whether that mix-up occurred on our side or theirs," the notes began. There was an air of exasperation in that first line, but Derrick couldn't tell why. Perhaps because of the air within this meeting.

"Harold, as someone who has been working closely on this project for the past two months, I do not think that would be the correct approach," Ericka assured.

"We shouldn't just be approaching it. We should be conquering it. That is what we do here at Death, Inc. We conquer," Harold said emphatically. He had been listening to Tony Robbins on his commute into work, and while he didn't understand most of it, there were some parts that were starting to seep into his professional life. He thought it was for the best.

In many ways, he felt out of control, in a position he did not fully understand. Maybe he just had to act like he understood. Like he was the boss he knew he could be. That dress-the-part mentality.

"Harold, I wish that would work in this situation, but we need to work with them to figure out what happened here. It is equally possible that it is our fault as well, but we need to have an honest conversation with everyone about our processes, and what we can do to investigate. I'm not entirely sure what Dennis's processes are, for example." Ericka looked to Dennis as she said this.

"You don't need to check my work. I don't make mistakes. If I made a mistake, you would know," Dennis said, still looking at the wood laminate he was working to peel from the particle board surface.

"This seems like the kind of situation where it looks like you made a mistake. So should I just assume that it's your mistake, because it seems like it?"

"This is not the kind of mistake I'd make. It would have had to happen either with you guys or with them. This is not under me or Natalie, to be clear. We just execute what you tell us to." Dennis paused, laughed to himself, then turned to Derrick, "Not *actually* execute, to be clear. I feel like I have to make it clear after that news article that has been circling my feed lately. 'Death, Inc. Euthanizes People'. Love it."

Ericka's eyebrows raised. It was exactly what she feared would happen, but she didn't have the capacity in this meeting to address that. She had to knock one thing out at a time. She couldn't focus on that now. Right now, this was for the chickadee. Next, they'd tackle the social media slam.

"We can return to that later, but right now, we have to find out how to prove we didn't screw this one up. We need to go through our processes, on both sides."

Dennis smirked, bu it was clear his mind was elsewhere. Eyes pointed downward, unfocused.

"Unless you have a better idea, Dennis. I'm all ears."

"Actually, I just might. Can I borrow Derrick for that? I think it might be a two-person job."

Ericka looked at Derrick. This poor kid—there was no way he could retain all of this. Only Day 2. But his face looked clear. Unconcerned.

"I'd love to get to know your processes," Derrick said, wondering if he was agreeing to too much, but excited to see what Dennis did.

"Only if you're comfortable. It couldn't hurt," Ericka said, uncertain. "Derrick, let's still meet later today to talk about the social media stuff once you two are done, okay?" She wanted to keep a close eye on it.

Chapter 16

"We're not actually going to talk about my processes," Dennis said as they sat in his Buick. "You don't need to know my processes."

"I'm still not following why we can't talk about this in the office," Dennis said, fumbling for a seat belt only to find it had been cut out—just two stubs where the belt had been. In the belt buckle, there was still the buckle insert, cut right before the metal key.

"This is more important than the office. We need to talk about Anissa," Dennis said.

Fuck, Derrick thought. This would not go away. He wished he had never seen the folder. He wished there had been at least a bit more explanation from Ericka so he knew what he could and couldn't say. Anything would be helpful right now.

"Remember how I said 'she's going to die soon' just this morning? I think she knows she's going to die," Dennis said. "Let me explain. I was looking back in our files, and she was supposed to die last week. She was also supposed to die two months ago. Six months ago. Most notably, exactly one year ago. This is no coincidence. I need you to investigate this for me."

How was this only Day 2? Derrick wondered to himself. How did he find himself here, in an objectively simple job filled with incredibly complicated, high-stake caveats? At this point, he would have preferred being an underpaid mercenary.

"To be clear, I'm not asking you to do anything that would jeopardize your job. That's not what I'm asking. I don't want you to lose your job over this, kid. But I would like to get more insight so I know how I should proceed with my job. You get me?" Dennis asked.

"No, I get you. I hear you," Derrick said, but he wasn't sure if he did. Not entirely.

"I need you to keep an eye out and shadow whenever a Mortal Soul Number comes in, do you hear me?"

"Yeah, I think—"

"Okay, then tell Ericka you want to shadow her and see what she's doing. I don't think it's her, but I don't't' want Harold to be suspicious if you are only following him. He isn't the sharpest tool in the shed, but he'd probably figure out something was up if you never followed Ericka. If anything, because it would create more work—and he usually tries to avoid that."

"I think I get it, yeah. So what do you want me to watch out for?" Derrick tried to play it cool, but he already knew what he should watch out for. The one thing that he already agreed to keep hidden. The one thing he now had to actively keep from two people. The one thing that, before he knew any of this, he swore he'd keep a secret.

This is what he had wondered it'd be. Something top secret. Official government. But much like he assumed, the pay didn't come with the high level of secrecy this job required. It also didn't come with the credentials.

Shit.

"Cool. Let's hang out for a bit longer. Do you want to get some lunch or something? We could go to the Applebee's, down the street. Really the only restaurant in town," Dennis said as he put his key in the ignition. At that point, "no" wasn't really an answer.

To make it clear this wasn't a kidnapping, Derrick said, "Sure, sounds good."

"Cool. I don't really make a habit of hanging out with people in the office, but you seem like good people," he said—not necessarily looking at Derrick, but looking forward. Dennis turned on the audio.

Take it easy, take it easy, don't let the sound of your own wheels drive you crazy...

Quiet, muffled. If you were to put a number on it, from 1-25, it was probably at a 7.

"Shit, I love The Eagles. I'm not sure why everyone seems so ashamed to like them. They've got some of the best musicians all in that one band, and you can't tell me some of their songs don't get stuck in your head. 'Desperado' and 'Peaceful Easy Feeling' and 'Hotel California'? You're lying to yourself if you say you hate that song. That, right there, is a perfect song."

Dennis was still staring straight at the road, as if he were monologuing—making no motions toward any of this dialogue going towards Derrick, but Derrick nodded in agreement just the same. He didn't hate The Eagles. He kept his tone neutral.

When they got to Applebee's, the same hostess Derrick saw the previous night sat them at the same booth he and Anissa sat at. She said nothing, and Derrick said nothing. Not even a nod of acknowledgment. This time, Derrick simply ordered fries. Dennis ordered nothing, but took a sandwich out of his pocket as soon as she left.

Their conversation was nothing significant. Dennis talked about vacations he's been on, girls he's dated, places he's lived. Not in a way that was supposed to make Derrick feel in any way less superior, but in a longing way—as if he had missed telling these stories, as if he was reliving them as he told them, as if he was grateful for Derrick's captive audience.

Derrick? Derrick was thrilled to have such an engaging one-way conversation so he, again, didn't accidentally say anything about the folder.

When they got back in the car, the end of "Take It Easy" wrapped up and "Witchy Woman" started playing.

Raven hair and ruby lips

Sparks fly from her fingertips

Echoed voices in the night

She's a restless spirit on an endless flight

"Ah, this classic. Underrated." Other than that, Dennis said nothing.

This time, they drove in silence, but it was a comfortable silence. After Dennis got all his stories out, and Derrick reacted with interest, they had come to some sort of understanding over that lunch. Not a solid friendship, not anything as concrete as that. But an understanding where silences weren't filled with uncertainty, and if they didn't speak for the next 10 years, it wouldn't bother either of them. Just that mutual understanding.

It wasn't until they got to the parking lot that Dennis said anything. This time, he turned to Derrick and put his hand on his shoulder. His hand gloved his shoulder, like a gorilla's hand holding a banana. Disproportionate.

"Hey, and about the Anissa thing. I'm serious when I say don't get too close. I understand she seems cool and you probably don't know each other all that well yet, but it's going to happen soon. I wanted to let you know to warn you, but also as a work warning. This kind of thing tends to . . . come up in our line of work often," Dennis paused, took his hand off Derrick's shoulder and ran his hand through his black hair.

"I've been in your position before, and I can tell you firsthand—it's just not fun, Derrick. There's some . . ." Dennis paused again, shifting his hands from his lap to the steering wheel to crossing them across his chest. "There's always some sort of guilt if you get to know them, even if you are 100% certain you're just going about the natural order of things."

Derrick paused. He understood what Dennis was saying. It registered in his brain, but hung there in the air, as if waiting to be let in by the other things he was hiding.

"And I realize that's a lot to take in, and I'm sorry for getting heavy, but I wish someone would have told me the first time it happened to me. It doesn't get easier, but you do learn ways of coping and dealing with it in time," Dennis continued.

This knowing knocked on the edges of Derrick's skull, as if he couldn't fully let it in until he took a moment to recognize his current realities—the ones all running in parallel. One where he knew Anissa would die but he couldn't tell her. One where he knew there was a folder keeping Anissa alive, but that she'd continue to get brutally injured until she was finally allowed to pass on, until nature finally was allowed to take its course. One where his life was completely normal, and he was just trying to make a friend at work.

He wished that the final one, that reality he constructed, was his only life. And up until two days ago, he would have thought that. Sure, he always was struggling financially, but he could have eventually disclosed that to his new friend. Those lives could have combined.

These lives, no matter how deep he got into either of them, could never collide. If they did in any sort of meaningful way, they would all explode.

Derrick began to process it all, but not fully. Not even close. There was still . . . that block. He'd have to wait until he got back to his office.

"I'm sorry, I have to get back to a meeting," Derrick said. He wasn't sure what else to say, or how else to end this, but he knew that he had to reconcile these thoughts in his head. Or at least begin to. Or escape them, even if only for a moment.

"Of course. I'm sorry for getting heavy. Let's do this more often though, hey? I don't have a lot of friends in the office, and I think this could be helpful for both of us."

"Sure, sure."

"Let's make it a regular thing," Dennis said, resting his gorilla hand on Derrick's small shoulder once more, like a father congratulating his son after a T-ball game.

"You bet," Derrick said before he could process what he said.

Derrick passed Anissa as he walked into the building, but luckily, she was helping someone else.

***

Ericka waited for Derrick to get back to the office, shut the door, and have time to open his laptop, before she burst in. She shut the door behind her, and in a hushed tone, asked, "You didn't tell him about the folder, did you?"

"What?" Derrick took a minute to process. He shook his head and shut his computer completely. "No. No, I didn't tell him. We didn't talk about that stuff, really."

Ericka's shoulders visibly relaxed as she said, "Oh, God. Phew. Good. I was scared he would try to get it out of you, or something. You didn't talk about the chickadee thing at all though? Really?"

Derrick ignored her question. "Does he know about it, do you think?" Derrick asked, as if he had never heard Dennis was suspicious of their department. Playing dumb.

Ericka took a seat across from his desk and crossed her legs, leaning over as if they were having a secret meeting.

"I probably shouldn't drag you into this so early, but I hope you don't mind that we're here now. I've wondered about Dennis recently." She paused as if she was going to elaborate, but she didn't. The air hung after her sentence for a beat before she looked back up at Derrick, as if to ask for his read on the situation.

He fumbled with his words before saying, "We mostly talked about personal stuff. His vacation to Bruges was something we talked a lot about. I've always been interested in Bruges." This was a lie. Derrick had never been interested in Bruges. Another layer to this triple life he was leading.

"Phew. This is such a relief. Phew," Ericka said. "I thought for sure he was trying to pull something out of you."

"Nope," Derrick lied.

"Okay, well, let me know if you need anything else today. Those newspaper articles Harold sent you. . .they're a lot. But maybe they'll give you some context. There are no action items there, but if you're curious on some of our troubles in the past, that's a pretty good summary of where we come from."

"Cool, sounds good." Derrick wondered if he should be saying anything else. If now he was suspicious because he wasn't saying anything. "I'll get right on that." He tried to continue the thought, but he had nothing left.

Until he remembered Dennis's request—to shadow whenever a soul needed to be processed. Derrick cleared his throat just as Ericka turned her back and asked, "Do you think I could shadow whenever a soul comes in? Just for training purposes? I'm sure I'll have to do it at some point, so it'd be nice to see it done as much as possible."

Ericka gave him a thumbs up as she left. In his mind, these different worlds were like a choose-your-own adventure. The more he said yes to one side, the deeper entrenched in that storyline he'd get, leaving the others shallower.

But in this path he's chosen, he's said yes to all three. He is not giving away the folder to Anissa or Dennis. And he is going to shadow Harold and Ericka as they process souls, to ensure Dennis doesn't get suspicious.

But would he end up telling him anything if he saw anything?

Was this *yes* to all sustainable?

This was all too much for Day 2—3:00 pm on Day 2. He didn't know what else to do but get some coffee, which would inevitably fuel his anxiety even more.

Chapter 17

The next day. Anissa got to the office early, as she liked to do. She was driving herself this time, a Buick she borrowed from Stephanie—not because it was the safe option, but because Gary and Stephanie couldn't drive her and there were no taxis, Lyfts or Ubers in Schuester. She took two aspirins and hoped for the best, and it seemed to help, at least for the drive there.

She could feel her torso shifting differently, as if her bone structure was altering itself around the injury—reallocating tasks to different, lesser-used muscles and ligaments. She wondered if her body would warp irreparably, if it would twist, contort, then stay that way, as parents warned of children making goofy faces. Underneath her fall coat and her sweater, she could feel the swelling and the bruising, though lessened, throbbing still. Changing. Shifting. Morphing as her body attempted to heal itself, while not giving it any time to rest.

She focused on keeping her body still as she grabbed her purse, slinging over the shoulder opposite from her injury and grabbing her travel mug with the other hand, filled with chai tea. She would normally have coffee in her mug, but she noticed her movements were more jittery when she had higher levels of caffeine. She wanted to ensure her movement stayed smooth.

Breathe in, breathe out, she told herself before sliding her body out of the car as controlled as possible, trying not to move her torso. Success.

But the wind.

The wind turned her shoulder-length hair into an impenetrable, sentient curtain that refused to escape her face. This lasted for about 30 seconds before the wind subsided.

Sun. No clouds. 50 degrees.

This was Anissa's type of weather. Had she not been severely injured, or had she not had work today, she'd probably be out hiking somewhere. Wherever she could find. Perhaps a park two hours out of town, one she had visited with Gary and Stephanie when she first moved here three years ago. For a moment, she lost herself in the woods they escaped to three years ago—the narrow dirt trails made narrower by overgrowth.

As she approached the door, she saw a piece of paper resting against it—as if someone had propped it there.

Was this the note she was hearing so much about? The note she heard people talking about as they came in, but rarely elaborated on?

She had never seen it, but it always seemed to appear just after she arrived. She never saw a person leaving the note, which was strange, because the doors were glass. There were no obstructions blocking her view. She looked around to see if maybe someone was still around—someone unfamiliar scurrying away in the distance. No one.

Odd.

She lowered herself using her knees as soon as she got to the door, keeping her torso as still as she could as she rested her things on the concrete ground—careful as she reached out toward it, careful to not lean too far close to it.

It was folded in half, a piece of paper from what looked to be a small, pocket-sized notebook. Aged paper.

Help me, it said.

What the fuck? was the first thing that came to her mind. *Surely, this can't be the note everyone is talking about, with so little urgency that this note clearly required.*

Instead of leaving the note there, she put the note in her bag, an exterior pocket where she knew it'd be easy to find. Situated her things once more, and lifted herself up with a stiff torso.

Who could she even ask about this? Who did she even know? She walked toward her desk in autopilot, her legs guiding her as her mind continued to unwind all hypotheses and conclusions in front of her like that giant choose-your-own-adventure.

She knew she had to tell someone. But who could she trust?

There was the janitor, but what would he do with that information? He seemed to know as much as she did, which was absolutely nothing.

Derrick, she suddenly thought. *Of course—I can email Derrick about this. He might know what to do.*

She logged into her computer, opened up her Outlook, and started a draft to Derrick. Her hands hovered over the keyboard.

How do you even begin to ask about this without sounding absolutely insane?

Hi Derrick,

I'm incredibly worried about what I've found this morning and was wondering if you'd have a look.

No, too emotional. Don't lead with emotions. Just lead with actions. Keep it simple, Anissa.

Hi Derrick,

See attached. If you have any questions, please see me directly.

She took a picture of the note and attached it as an image to the email.

Perfect. That's all he needed. Send.

Chapter 18

"So, what did you think of the articles I sent to you?" Harold asked Derrick. Today was Day 3. It was 7:45 am. In Derrick's hand was a cup of coffee. With Harold, a bag lunch. Derrick could smell it, but couldn't quite figure out what it was. Something pickled—that was all he could gather. To him, pickled was not a great smell, but he tried to hide that from his face. He always felt guilty when his sensitive sense of smell betrayed him. He contorted his face in an attempt to hide the unavoidable disgust he felt.

"Thank you for sending those to me." Derrick's voice was stilted, suffocated by the smell. "I'm still going through them, but it does give a lot of backstory on the company as a whole." He coughed to hide his discomfort, an involuntary tick.

"So, how do you think we should respond to them?" Harold said, as if he were saying something easy. Like *How are we going to pick up all of the napkins you've just dropped on the floor*? or something akin to that.

Derrick paused. "Respond to *all* of them? I don't think that would be wise." He tried to sound polite, but it was difficult to hide the doubt in his voice, on top of everything else.

"But Ericka said Reddit is talking about them. Don't you think we should at least acknowledge them?" Harold asked.

The elevator doors opened, revealing a casual Harold and an already stressed Derrick.

On the other side was Ericka, as she always seemed to be when the elevator door opened. As if she were an NPC, a side character in a video game waiting on the other side of the door. As if her story was on pause until the active player came into the scene.

"Oh, God. What is that smell? Is that pickled fish?" Ericka said before she could even say hello. Her face twisted, an immediate gut repulsion. She had smelled that before, but it didn't feel right to say when there was just one person. When there were two people in the elevator, at least both could deflect on the other silently.

The air of *we know who it is, but we don't have to say it* is much less obtrusive and offensive when there are two people instead of one.

Neither of them said anything.

Both of them went to their offices. Derrick with his coffee. Harold to get settled, then to go get his coffee.

Derrick tried to log into Reddit, but it was blocked.

He couldn't even investigate it if he tried. Was he even allowed to look it up at home, given the "no work from home, all work stays in office" policy?

What was Harold talking about? Derrick wondered, but he decided to file that away into a note he wrote down. "Ask Ericka about Reddit." That should cover it.

And that's when he saw it. The notification in his inbox.

Subject: "Re: Soul received."

It was the only thing the subject said—no body, outside of Ericka's response saying "I've got this one."

Derrick hadn't gotten the original email, Ericka had manually CC'd him on her response, but that was something he'd also have to address later. He added it to his note, right below Reddit.

When Ericka didn't immediately burst in, Derrick decided to wait outside of his own office. If anything, he had to look like he was keeping an eye on the soul intake process. If he missed the first one, Dennis would probably understand, right?

This was only his third day. How was this only his third day?

"Oh, good. You're here. Let's go. Should be quick," Ericka said as she checked her phone, filled with notifications. Derrick struggled to keep up with her as she walked, though he was taller than her. *Left, right, left, right, leftrightleftrightleftright* down the stairwell—eight floors down without a word.

Similar to the last time, but this time, there was this sense of purpose. It always seems less awkward when there is urgency, when the mind is able to deviate toward different things.

"You kind of remember the process from last time, right?" Ericka said as she punched the code into the door.

She checked her phone again, then shoved it in her back pocket.

"One thing I left out is that you have to make sure it's valid before you take the receipt. Sometimes, the email notification is in error. Sometimes, the tech side misfires, then *oops*—you're accidentally taking someone's soul away and giving it to someone else."

"But you don't have to worry about that, yet. I'll be here with you through the process for at least the first few times you do it, and that won't be for another month."

Souls accidentally being stolen? That seems like something he should tell Dennis. Or did Dennis already know about that? He didn't seem the sentimental type on the surface, but if he knew the person—

"Do you remember the first step, outside of checking if it's an error?" Ericka asked.

"Receipt, in the first machine, over there." Derrick pointed to the machine furthest to the left. "Match that number up with the number within the first folder, and that's where you grab the name."

"Perfect. You've got this. You'll be a pro in no time." Ericka paused and looked at the number.

Derrick looked over her shoulder, but not intrusively so. The number was shorter than the numbers Derrick had seen. Only four digits. *8213*.

"This one's a bit of a controversial one. I can bring you up to speed once we get upstairs, but the process is slightly simplified. Not as precise," Ericka said as she went through the numbers in the first folder. "You always have to double check, but to my knowledge, this is definitely an animal's soul."

"What kind of animal?" Derrick surprised even himself with this question. He was surprised his first question wasn't *what* or *why* or *what the fuck*, but at this point, so much information had already been thrown at him, it wasn't that shocking.

"Some kind of bird, from what I'm seeing. I know that because it starts with an 8," she said, as if this was a perfectly logical explanation. When she saw Derrick's blank face, she clarified. "There's an additional list at the back that lists the animal numbers, but you get used to the codes."

"Is that where the chickadee mix-up—"

"I want to make it clear that we're not taking full blame for that," Ericka turned to look at him, pausing her work, folder in hand. "But it's possible that's what happened, yes," she said as soon as she turned her back away from him again.

"Got it. We can talk about this later, if that works better," Derrick said, noting her rush.

Ericka didn't respond. She continued to go from folder to folder, checking each number and paper before she finally printed something out from the second machine and stapled it to a piece of paper in the final folder. She placed the folder in the *Out* basket.

"I think Dennis might have a better idea of what happened there with the chickadee," Ericka said, giving no additional context. "He might be a better person to work with on that, if I were to take a guess." She didn't say this with any hostility in her tone—just a simple nudge.

He wasn't sure how to proceed within all these paths that continued to intersect at random, without any sort of warning.

"Well, that's that. Let's go upstairs now, yeah? It sounds like Harold gave you quite a bit to look at. I have some things for you, too, if Harold's stuff is too overwhelming. I realize it's only your third day, so I want to be sure you're not completely out in the middle of the ether without a paddle, if you know what I mean."

Derrick had never heard that phrase before, but he knew what she meant.

There was total silence again between both going up the stairwell, but this time, it was back to awkward. When they were three floors up, they met the same pace—but Derrick forced himself to slow down, so they weren't walking next to each other, stair by stair, in silence.

There's something about being a few steps behind someone that allows you to be in your own thoughts. If you're not sharing the same stair, you're allowed to be silent. Same stairs, though? Must acknowledge. Like if you make eye contact in an elevator.

Once they reached the top of the stairwell, Ericka turned to him and said, "You let me know again if you have any questions today, okay? I have a busy day again, but I'll be able to answer if you need me."

***

Derrick opened his computer to see two new recurring calendar invites.

Anissa for every Monday evening. Dennis for every Tuesday afternoon.

Great. Excellent. Wonderful. As if he didn't have enough anxiety already.

Next, an email from Harold that had three more news articles attached to them. There was still no body to the email providing any sort of context or explanation. Just articles.

1995: "PETA Protests Death, Inc."

1996: "Can You Predict Death? One Former Death, Inc. Employee Thinks So!"

1996 (again): "But What Is Death, Inc., Really?"

Derrick looked at these articles in conjunction with the ones Harold had sent yesterday. They hadn't had anything written on them since 1996, until now.

What happened between 1996 and now? Why the gap?

He noticed an email from Anissa as well, but he flagged it for later. He had to address the current tasks, then he would look at her email. He couldn't intersect these lives completely, not yet. He'd have to compartmentalize them. He'd wait until later.

It was only Day 3, but he already felt as if he were under water. The water kept rising as more things appeared, unfolded. And he already wasn't great at multi-tasking—more of a one-track-mind deep thinker, but he tried his best to block these things into manageable chunks. The reverse problem, compared to his data entry job—there, it was monotony. Now, he longed for that monotony.

His mind went back to Harold's email as he replied, CCing Ericka.

"Thank you for these," Derrick typed in response to Harold's email. "Is there a reason there is a 12-year gap between the last news article and the most recent? Have there been any other accounts of Death, Inc. in the news?"

Derrick didn't want to make it sound like he was admonishing Harold, or telling Harold he was incompetent, but he wanted to be sure he wasn't missing anything.

To clear the air, he ended the email with "Respectfully, Derrick."

Respectfully, as it usually is in emails, was an overstatement. But it seemed right at the time.

Almost immediately, he got a reply, "No, but thank you for checking. Please let me know what your plan is to address these. Thanks much, Harold"

Well, okay then, Derrick thought. At least that made his job less cumbersome.

He opened a Google Doc and started creating ideas:

"Death, Inc.: What are we really?"

No that doesn't work.

"The Natural Lifecycle of a Soul"

No, that made him sound . . . well, not reputable, especially given the topic he would be writing on.

Suddenly, Dennis leaned in the frame of his open office door. "Hey, did you get my calendar invite?"

Had it been open the whole time? He was so sure he had closed it, but he also hadn't heard Dennis come in at all. No creak of the door. No footsteps. Nothing.

"Yep, it's on the calendar."

"Great, great. That's wonderful." But instead of leaving, he closed the door behind him and sat down in the chair across from Derrick, crossing his legs. "I saw there was a death that went through this morning. It went through all right, didn't it? I think I saw it go through smoothly."

"Oh, the bird? Yeah, yeah, that was Ericka—"

"That was a test. I wanted to see if you would shadow her."

"What?"

"That was just a red-winged blackbird. Their souls are expendable. Just a red-winged blackbird. Half of them don't have souls to begin with, so I'm sure this one wouldn't miss a soul too much."

"I'm not following . . ." Derrick looked up at Dennis, and leaned over his desk. "You're saying we stole the soul of a red-winged blackbird just to see if I'd keep my word?"

"You'll understand how minor of a thing that is once you get the hang of this."

Derrick paused, and doubted that he would ever think this was something minor. "You're saying you stole a soul just to see if I'd do something I said I would?"

"You're leaving out that it's a *red-winged blackbird's* soul—which, again, once you get used to this place, you'll know is really not an issue. Again, that red-winged blackbird with a soul was an anomaly. They usually don't have those. I doubt he'll miss it. It's not like I took a puppy's soul. That would be catastrophic."

"Is this what happened to the chickadee?"

Dennis paused, face flushed. “No—no, no. That’s not what happened to the chickadee. Though we should probably talk about that too, before we go any further. Not now, but eventually.”

Derrick returned his gaze to the computer, speechless. He looked at the article. “PETA Protests Death, Inc.” and wondered what they’d think about this now, 22 years later. He could see their new article now—“Death, Inc. Treats Red-Winged Blackbirds as Expendable” or “Death Inc. Is Systematically Removing Souls From Red-Winged Blackbird Population.”

But the problem was that Derrick had no idea how much had actually changed since then. He couldn’t seem to get a straight answer from anyone about anything that went on around here. All he knew was that it was his job to make sure they were saving face. That, when things happened, he would come up with the words to somehow make all of their problems go away.

What if this got out? This had to be a very minor thing. This for sure wasn’t the first time Dennis did something like this. Based on his posture alone, slacked, relaxing into the backrest, he had definitely done something much worse before and gotten away with it.

But what?

“Maybe it's something I'm misunderstanding, but this seems like something I should be worried about.”

“Who would notice? Those birds are assholes, anyway.” Dennis said. “But I’m glad you’re with me on this.”

“I’m just not fully understanding what just happened to the red—”

“I understand your stance on the red-winged blackbird, Derrick." His tone, annoyed.

“It’s just that this is the exact kind of thing that would—”

“What is more important is that *now* I know you have my back, right? You’re going to keep an eye out for anything that looks fishy?” Dennis interrupted talking loudly to drown out Derrick's words.

But this—this right here was fishy, Derrick thought to himself. This man sitting across the table from him removed the soul from a living bird with little thought.

“So, you do know what happened with the chickadee.” Derrick switched subjects.

“We can talk about it later. I’ll tell you, eventually, if you promise to keep it a secret. You can’t tell anyone, especially not Ericka. You know how she gets about these things.”

Derrick sighed. *Add it to the list of things to not talk about.*

Dennis continued. “But you’re still going to keep an eye on them for me, right? Make sure everything’s running smoothly?”

“As long as this doesn't happen again—”

"I promise this won't happen again," Dennis said, full eye contact.

"Okay," Derrick said, "I'll help you out." His tonw was still unsure.

“Cool.” Dennis paused, looked down, uncrossed his legs, and pushed himself out of the chair. “Well, that’s all I really needed to talk about, unless you need anything from me.”

“Nope, I’m good.”

“All right. Well, I’ll see you around.” They stared at each other for what felt like an hour before Dennis left.

The door shut with a *thud,* and the air emptied. Derrick sighed.

Now, he was waiting to hear from Ericka that he had to watch out for Dennis. That he’d have to do intel on Dennis for suspected wrongdoing. *That would be the end of me,* he figured. One layer too far. But he didn’t put it past this current experience. Just when you don’t think things will get any worse, somehow, the world surprises you. As if, as soon as you ask that question, fate or karma or whatever you prescribe to comes out with a hot new banger just to throw you off a bit.

It builds character Derrick heard his Grandpa Al's voice echo in his head.

But at least Dennis was honest. He was grateful for that. Sometimes painfully honest, but at least Derrick knew what was happening with him.

Derrick returned to his Google Doc.

How to address all the articles Harold had just sent him.

He would have to keep it vague. This was partly to ensure he wasn't reminding people what they had done, but also because he still wasn't 100% sure what they were doing, and where their control rested. Were they truly able to steal souls, or is it difficult? Are there any safety procedures in place outside of an archaic folder structure?

Have they done anything great, notably great? Derrick paused and wrote that down in his notebook under the header, "Questions to Ask."

"Death, Inc.—What Is It?"

This was his working title—not something he'd stick with, but it was a start. It seemed that most of the troubles came from people not knowing what they did, who they are, or what they hope to accomplish.

While they had made some mistakes, surely those mistakes would look less glaring if people had a small idea of what happened behind closed doors.

Right?

Outside of this red-winged blackbird thing.

And outside of the chickadee thing.

And outside of . . . whatever else there was.

But how many of these things were public knowledge?

How much did they know about where they stood? What could he say, and what would be taboo?

He had no idea. He could barely wrap his head around it. Any of it.

He found himself longing, again, for a spreadsheet. Any spreadsheet. Data entry. Something mindless. Simple. Predictable.

Chapter 19

Anissa opened Derrick's email the moment it hit her inbox.

Anissa:

When you picked up that note, was there a chickadee waiting nearby? I think I might know what this is about, but I can't talk about it yet . . . hope you understand.

Her eyes crept carefully over each word. "Chickadee?" she said out loud. "What the fuck is he talking about?" she muttered. She drew her face closer to the screen, as if the closeness would change the words so they'd make more sense.

No such luck. None of it made sense. "Hope you understand" he said, while providing no explanation, like a fucking psychopath.

Does he think I'm stupid?

Settle down, Anissa, she thought to herself, trying to calm herself down. She often thought people thought the worst of her in these types of situations, as if she was at fault for his shitty explanation.

It was in these moments she was happy she never got a prescription for oxycodone. All she wanted to be was numb, emotionally and physically. The aspirin was beginning to wear off, and she could feel the dull, pulsing throb to a sharp pain again. She felt her muscles reacting to the pain happening in her abdomen, and it showed visibly on her face.

She wanted to get up and check if there was a chickadee, like Derrick had mentioned in his email, but she couldn't. She couldn't risk getting out of her chair and falling. The pain was growing worse—more debilitating, more incapacitating.

She needed this job. She couldn't afford the rest required to properly heal—time wise or money wise. She had to work through it and hope her body properly mended itself, despite all odds.

But she was certain she hadn't noticed a chickadee at the time. She would have made note of it. They were her favorite birds.

She replied.

Derrick:

No, no chickadee that I saw. What's this about anyway? Sounds weird.

Derrick responded within 10 seconds.

Anissa:

You have no idea. I'll come down to pick up the note over my lunch.

***

Did Derrick want to see Anissa? No, not particularly. Not because she wasn't great to talk with. That wasn't it at all.

But all these things shoved straight in his face all morning—he could feel his filters eroding, the stress churning in his chest. The stress broke down the barriers between his two worlds: what he wanted to do and what he needed to do.

But he knew he had to. He had to see the note for himself, to tell everyone what was happening. He was grateful that she reached out to him, sure, but why are these notes still happening? What does that mean?

He took the stairs. He passed New Beginnings gathered near the door the seventh floor, where he unintentionally joined Susan for a few flights. She nodded to him when she saw both of them going the same way, but she remained silent until the fifth floor.

"Gotta use the stairs more often. Gotta make sure to get these steps in. We do too much sitting!" Susan said as she exited the fifth floor.

Derrick was grateful for the now-empty stairwell. *Time to think.*

But as soon as your mind is given time to think, it begins to unravel. When it begins to dissect every single possible potential. Every single possible thing that could go wrong.

What if I accidentally tell her to be careful, and she asks why I say that, and I don't have an answer? Derrick thought. That was something he could see himself doing.

It's just really stressful keeping on top of all of this. What if she pressed and asked him to elaborate? Would he break?

Derrick genuinely wanted to be Anissa's friend, but there was no way to be friends in this situation. As soon as he started to get personal, all of this would begin to unravel. His alter-worlds were all-consuming. There was no escaping them. He'd have to hide them behind doors completely when he was around her.

Or, what if she asked anything about the chickadee he already told her about?

Christ.

His heart. His heart was beating out of his chest. Sweat. Panic sweat, distinctive smell. Sour. Strong.

First floor. He hung behind the door until he heard footsteps from the other side of the door. Someone approached.

"Excuse me," a man he didn't recognize held the door, shuffling his body as he tried to adjust it so it wasn't awkward for Derrick to get by him.

Derrick did that half-walk, half-jog and waved to thank him—the kind some people do when they try to cross the street without being an inconvenience.

“Hey, you okay?” the voice said from behind him. “You don’t look all that hot.”

“Yeah, I’m fine. Just a long walk from the eighth floor,” Derrick said, walking toward Anissa, who had already turned in his direction. Stiff. Her face was pained, but her posture was urgent. In her hand she was holding the note—small, crinkled.

On it, "HELP ME."

“So, what is this about a chickadee?” Anissa said as soon as she was sure he was within earshot. She didn’t want to give him a moment to lead into it. She just wanted an answer, straight. If anything, she wasn’t sure how long she wanted to continue talking. Talking, breathing—everything hurt. And after taking aspirin for so long, it didn’t dull like it used to, but she knew taking anything heavier would be disastrous with her addictive family history. She tried to keep her composure.

But Derrick could not. He felt like he was stuck inside the beginning of that Eminem song—*palms are sweaty, knees weak, arms are heavy*—except without the spaghetti. His face was flushed. His heart pounded. He could feel it, and he tried to breathe in, then out, slowly. But he couldn’t stop it. He tried clearing his throat, to buy time, but it didn’t give him much—half a second, tops.

She noticed. How couldn’t she?

“You know you can tell me, right? It’s not like I’m going to narc on you. Who would I tell anyway?” Anissa tried to whisper, but somehow, this hurt worse. Something about using more effort to whisper, something about leaning in for effect.

Derrick froze. “It’s just part of a project I’m working on now. It’s not important. Just needed to know—”

“It’s just so strange because it’s so specific, you know? You’d have to know I’d ask, right? Especially with a note like this?” Anissa held the note up between her pointer and middle fingers. It folded in the middle, folding over the tip of her middle finger.

“It’s just a joke. Don’t even worry about it. It’s not a big—”

"I know this has been happening a lot. I've heard people talking about it. I know it's not a joke." This was a lie. She had been hearing things about it, but she didn't know for sure that he wasn't joking. All she had was a hunch.

But she usually trusted her gut with these kinds of things.

Derrick took a breath. "Okay, it's a project I'm working on. Something to do with souls."

Souls? Anissa paused. Maybe this had something to do with the newspaper article her mother sent her the past week:

"DEATH, INC. EUTHANIZES PEOPLE."

It was the one that had been explained away by everyone she brought it to as, "Well, yeah, your predecessor was something, that's for sure. We're so happy to have someone like you. Someone more trustworthy."

But trustworthy with what? With what information? She knew nothing. Absolutely nothing. Nada. Zilch. Zip. When people asked her about the company she worked for, she had nothing. She usually said it is a local chain, but when people asked about the industry, she usually said something like "I'm still getting to know it. I'll let you know in a month!"

"What's the project?" she asked after a deafening silence. "What exactly is it you do up there?"

She didn't say this with an accusatory tone. She didn't want him to think she was drilling him. She tried to keep her tone curious, though in her gut, she knew there was something happening here. Something deeper.

"It just seems super strange that you'd have such a specific question after I tell you about this note," she said, hanging on that last word. She reached to hand him the note. "But if you think it's none of my business, then it's none of my business."

Derrick paused. Was he in the clear? Should he say something to smooth it over, or give her a bit of information? Surely, this wasn't completely classified. Surely, people outside of the department knew. Certainly, it would get back to her, eventually.

He took the note and looked down at it.

"Hey, thanks for thinking of me, though."

Anissa watched him walk away with the note. She was thinking about him now, wondering what it all could mean. How could a chickadee possibly fit into that narrative?

She turned her body carefully, inch by inch, focusing on moving each muscle separately to maximize control over the pain. No more aspirin. She should have brought more. *Is that healthy? How many aspirins can one take in a day?*

She swore she saw a chickadee hovering by the front door, but maybe it was her eyes seeing what was on her brain. Imagining things and putting pieces together that didn't exist.

She wrote down in her notebook: *Souls + Chickadee + HELP ME!* She shut it immediately, as if it would give her away if someone saw it. No one could know what she was looking for.

But why?

Again, just a gut feeling.

She made a mental note to start really looking into Death, Inc.—nothing skimmed or surface level.

But only when her pain subsided.

Derrick's gut, on the other hand, was about to explode. As was his chest. As was his brain.

A headache. A chest ache. His entire body ached from the stress this job was giving him, already. His muscles ached from the constant tensing. His brain hurt from the constant overanalyzing.

He didn't expect to have to deal with this amount of pressure in his first week. Was there any sort of holding period where he could still comfortably say *no, thank you* to this job, where he could just dip out?

His mother told him to give it a chance last night when he called her, but he also kept most of it from her. Her heart was not doing well, and he didn't want to make it worse.

He gave her a sanitized version, saying he was working PR for a new local T-shirt printing company start-up, so it makes sense why her answer was vague. He only gave her vague details.

He could hear his grandfather's voice in his head—*what, it can't be that hard if there are set hours.* This is what he said when Derrick complained about his job at Subway back in high school, before he dove into a story about how he used to work in the coal mines. Or maybe it was on a farm. Or was he a butcher?

Derrick couldn't remember. After a while, all the stories seemed to mesh. After someone passes, it's difficult to remember the exact things they said as time begins to tarnish them.

Derrick's mind focused back. There had to be some good he could do in this job.

But where?

Where could he do any sort of good within this organization without giving it a complete overhaul? Where could he begin?

He looked at the note again.

How a chickadee found a pen and paper and the dexterity to write a note was beyond him, but desperate times often bring out the best in souls—and Derrick imagined this human soul trapped in a chickadee's body was more desperate than he could ever comprehend from within his human-soul, human-body experience.

For a moment, he related with the chickadee, or at least how he imagined the chickadee must be feeling. Though, admittedly, its plight seemed much more horrific.

Derrick opened his computer again to check his email.

Nothing.

Nothing of importance, that is. Dennis sent him a GIF of a silverback gorilla dancing in a circle about five minutes ago set at high importance, but other than that, nothing was actually important.

The article.

The article he'd have to write for Death, Inc. exonerating Death, Inc. What would he say?

He returned to his Google Doc, revising its title:

"Death, Inc.—What Is It, Really?"

He typed, then read what he wrote in his head. *The shadows of Death, Inc. are not so much shadows as they are unknowns. What seems the scariest is often the most unknown.*

He deleted it when he sensed its tone. What did he mean by *scary*? And *unknown*? Double *unknowns*?

Another email popped up, breaking Derrick's thoughts. More news articles from Harold.

Derrick wasn't sure they were news articles, but he assumed as much when he saw an email with no subject line and several attachments.

He couldn't deal with that right now.

Writing had always been Derrick's stress reliever. That's why he went into studying English. When faced with the insurmountable number of options and an unfathomable amount of debt, all he wanted to do was write. That was all he could force himself to do.

A blank sheet was always more therapeutic than anything else he's tried.

But this? What good would exonerating Death, Inc. do?

This blank page didn't hold possibilities. It only held all his fears and his anxieties—a moral quandary. What had he signed up for?

***

Ericka rushed to Death, Inc.'s basement as soon as she arrived the next day. She didn't ask Derrick to go with her because, well, she needed her space, and she wanted a moment to herself in the basement. She thought about it. She did. He hasn't been here that long, and he really seems interested in what's happening.

It wasn't as much of a hurry as she often made it out to be. The hurry was unnecessary, but it had become a part of the charade. *The hurry to pass a soul on to be recycled.* It was not lost on her that they didn't have anyone doing this nights and weekends or holidays—and admittedly, that is when most of the deaths occur. Even the animal ones.

It was something she had constructed earlier in her time here. When she noticed that receipts often piled up until the end of the month, or until another birth happened and there were no more souls to recycle. As part of her process improvement, Ericka invented a reason to hurry to ensure this wouldn't happen again. To ensure that souls were processed as soon as they came in, to avoid a huge amount of work at the end of the month. To make sure work was getting done incrementally.

"Things would not go as expected," is all she told Harold, and he seemed to buy that. Not only buy that, but use it as a reminder for both him and her. "Things will not go as expected" he'd say, if it took even a minute for either of them to respond.

To be clear, it's not ideal if they wait. If they wait, there's always a chance the soul would reabsorb into a body well beyond repair—which is not ideal, and something they tried to avoid at all costs. Sure, they can pass on a soul after it's been reabsorbed, but with that brings extra risk, extra work, extra pain for the unwilling participant.

There were four receipts on the register: three animal and one human. She could tell by the numbers. Humans had longer soul IDs, and animals had shorter IDs, if they had any IDs at all. And sometimes, if a process hadn't been created for a species, or if they were still trying to discover if a species had a soul, it simply showed nothing. No ID. Just a blank receipt.

That was still up for debate—whether all animals had souls. Ericka liked to think they did. Not only because of her experience with pets growing up, but also because she couldn't fathom living without some sort of guidance—some sort of moral compass of right and wrong.

That's what a soul is, right? She wasn't entirely sure. After seven years of working directly with souls, even Ericka wasn't entirely sure how to define one.

She looked at the register. A rabbit. A racoon. A possum. A human.

New Beginnings liked to remind everyone that assuming an animal has a humanoid soul is a bit presumptuous. *Assuming that an animal's soul should be processed in the same way as a human's soul was a bit presumptuous too,* they stated emphatically.

The longer Ericka was here, the more she agreed with them. As much as she didn't want to agree with them, she agreed with them, even if she didn't want to say it outright.

To be clear, she wasn't saying animals didn't have souls. But perhaps there were things we would never understand, never be able to wrap our brains around. Much like how extraterrestrial life is often depicted—even in our fiction, an alien lifeform is always a distorted biped humanoid. A human with a twist. But the reality is probably even more distorted than our brains can comprehend, simply because we don't know what is possible outside of our own experience.

It seemed that most of the errors came from the animal souls they processed. There were often too many of them to process, and their process was not as fleshed out as the human soul process because, admittedly, they had no way of checking. When a baby is born without a soul, it's apparent—we inherently know how a baby acts, typically. We are much more equipped to tell if everything isn't working as expected when a human baby is born. But when something like a budgie is born without a soul, there is more of a question mark. And that's only if it's even noticed.

This chickadee thing was hanging on her mind. She knew there was something she was missing. Something grander than just a simple mistake. It would have to be a series of mistakes, or a glitch that had built up over time, or perhaps something else entirely. But what?

An unrecycled human soul, still containing the memories of its former self, somehow stuck in a bird—specifically, a chickadee. The fact that it was a chickadee was important, based on previous studies done within their company. It seemed less mistake, more suspect.

Or at least that's how it seemed, at least in her mind. If it still contained its memories, that would mean it would remember how to do very specifically human tasks, right? How else could it write, communicate, understand an office? A pen and paper?

She had been thinking about it all night.

Does a soul have memory, even after it's been recycled? Surely, you can't completely wash something clean. There will always be residue remaining, and even if that residue is microscopic, it will continue to build as more iterations pass.

Do those memories come back instinctively if pressed, remaining dormant until absolutely necessary? Or maybe if a soul is placed in the wrong vessel, does it reject, like an organ placed in the wrong blood type? What manifests when there is an error, and what wins—the body or the soul?

Or maybe it was a series of glitches manifesting into this one glitch. Perhaps one human soul that wasn't processed correctly somewhere down the line, so it went through several iterations until it landed in the wrong vessel. Less malleable than other souls she had encountered.

Or was it?

She had no idea.

She remembered reading about an experiment conducted on monkeys around 1920 where scientists were trying to physically identify where a human soul resides, and they thought it was in the brain. With that information, these scientists decided to sever the heads of monkeys and connect those heads to other monkey bodies—bodies that were not their own. They survived, on average, 48 hours. But from the scientific notes, it sounds like those 48 hours were a ghastly, terrifying, horrifying experience—one that only sociopaths would wish on their mortal enemies.

While there was no way to get a full account of what those monkeys endured, every note mentioned intense shock, confusion, fear, and the screams. The terror.

Was that what happened when the wrong soul was placed in the wrong body?

There had been experiments placing a human soul into an animal's body, but the notes within them were sparse, unhelpful. Unlike the monkey experiment, there was no common reaction listed.

She thought she had seen the chickadee this morning as she was walking in—the small chickadee body making surprisingly intense eye contact. Or, at least she thought it was. It's difficult to tell with their eyes.

But she was certain it was watching her as she opened, then shut the door behind her. It continued to watch her as she walked further into the lobby until it was out of sight.

Then, suddenly, she heard a knock on the door of the recycling room. Derrick. She saw his face from the glass window on the top of the door.

How did he know I was down here? she wondered. *Why is he here?* This seemed a bit more intense than simply wanting to know how things worked, or wanting to help. This seemed intrusive.

She tried to pass the thought. *This was still his first week. Maybe he's still eager.*

But there was something about this. What was he here to do, really?

"Hey, I didn't expect you to be here already." Ericka lied. She knew he was here. She hoped he didn't notice.

"It's cool, no worries. Just want to see what I can learn today," Derrick said. But there was something about the way he held himself as he said this—uncomfortably stiff posture. No slouch. As if he was line reading. And why was he sweating so much?

Did he run down the stairs to catch me? she thought. She would have to find a subtle way to ask him. Somehow.

***

Anissa got to work an hour early to pick up the note. It was the same as yesterday—"Help me!"—in scrawled penmanship.

Almost identical to the day before, but this time, it was on the back of a CVS Pharmacy receipt. The writing was simulated bold with what looked to be a BIC pen, gone over several times to make sure nothing got lost in translation.

She was hoping to be the first one in this morning, the first one to get the note. Sure, her side still hurt, and she needed rest, but she knew there was something to this.

Something didn't seem right. That persistent gut feeling.

Now, this time, she was *certain* she saw the chickadee hovering outside of the glass front door—looking directly at her as she held its note in her hand. It had to be from that chickadee.

It wasn't lost on Anissa how absolutely insane this sounded. Where would a bird get a pen? Paper, sure—people drop receipts and scraps of paper all the time. But pens? And how could it even write? Its feet? Is that impossible? The angle, I mean. Picture it. Try to picture it.

All of it seemed physically impossible.

Yet, as the chickadee hovered in front of the door, something about its insistence made it seem like this was the only plausible explanation.

And she now knew she couldn't ask Derrick, at least not outright. She'd have to get it out of him some other way.

She would have to find a way to ask him. Not outright—she would have to find a subtle way to get it out of him. Somehow.

***

"Did you get anything written yet?" Harold typed in his email to Derrick.

He didn't want to disturb Derrick in case he was in the middle of writing, but he also wanted to get a temperature gauge on it. He understood Derrick was a creative.

Harold knew creatives worked differently.

His wife, Sharon, was a creative herself, though her creativity of choice was mostly needlepoint. Birds, lately—she's been working on her shading specifically, which birds were excellent practice on. He knew it was best to not interrupt a creative when they're at work, especially if there's a needle involved.

But he was really counting on this. Relying on this.

He didn't question why he was relying on this, outside of the fact that he knew he *had* to rely on this. Outside of the fact that Ericka said they should get some PR support around the recent news article.

He still had the article on his desk, where he placed it the day Ericka came in to tell him they needed to hire someone new.

Was that only a week ago? It had to be longer than a week.

He looked at the date on the article, then looked at the date on his computer.

Then he looked at the article again.

"DEATH, INC. EUTHANIZES PEOPLE."

What would his father have done in this situation, when he was in this role before Harold? At their old facility, things were run quietly and efficiently. Nobody seemed to ask questions unless they had to, but their questions could usually be explained away rather easily.

The problem was people had too much time on their hands, now. Conversation was too easily accessible. That's what it was.

He stopped himself. He couldn't let himself get stuck in the past. He knew he was susceptible to that—when he listened to the radio lately, he noticed that he didn't understand the new music as he used to.

He didn't want to become that person. He wanted to remain malleable. Open to new things. Not moldable, but still able to change. Still able to find new things exciting.

But, as he bit into the same tuna sandwich Sharon made him every day, followed by the same Keebler cookies he ate—three of them, little elves in varying shapes of dysmorphia—this potential openness to change exhausted him. He did not want to understand anymore. His brain felt as if it had absorbed all it was meant to absorb in this lifetime, full capacity.

Before pressing *send*, Harold added, "No rush."

Keep it cool, Harold, he thought to himself. *Even if you can't be cool anymore, at least you can keep your tone cool.*

Derrick got three emails in rapid succession—one from Ericka, one from Anissa, and one from Harold. *Beep. Beep. Beep.* Within five seconds. Uncomfortably uncanny.

***

Anissa didn't see the chickadee until she heard it tapping on the glass. At first the tap was faint, then slightly more insistent. She assumed it was a branch at first, when the back of her mind processed it, until she heard three insistent taps on the glass.

When she looked up, she saw it. The chickadee hovered in front of the door, its eyes looking at her, piercing. Probing. As if it was waiting for an answer she, and only she, could provide.

She looked around her. No one. Not one person in the lobby.

It was always a slight risk after lunch—what, with people selectively coming in and out as they please, as if lunch is a marker of when it is acceptable to start talking about leaving.

But she figured she had a good 15-minute window right now.

She didn't know why she needed to get up and address the chickadee at the door, but there seemed no other options. This was the key, the direct key to all her questions. The note. The purpose. The reason.

She shifted her weight as she stood, wondering if soon it would become muscle memory to stand with the least amount of pain if she never fully recovered. If her muscles would just get stronger in different areas.

As it saw her walking toward it, the bird tapped again, as if to prove it had made the sound—as if to say *you're not going crazy* despite the rest of the scene appearing, well, absolutely surreal.

"I'll be there in a second," she said under her breath, as if the chickadee was already exhausting her, though she was more than interested in what it would say. She was more annoyed with her own circumstances, her own forced slow pace—nothing outside of herself. She was more talking to herself under her breath, as if to slow her heart rate and get herself to think rationally before approaching what was sure to be a situation that, in any other context, would be incomprehensible.

She held her side and winced as she opened the heavy door. The chickadee looked back at her as it flew up and down, as if it were stuck between two panes of glass.

This is foolish. I'm being ridiculous. It's just a bird, Anissa thought to herself, but just as she was about to close the door again, the chickadee pecked at her arm.

It hadn't been moving up and down at random—it had been trying to show her something. Guiding her in a certain direction.

"So, I should follow you?" Anissa said to the bird, slow. *Could it understand what I was saying? It wrote in English, but could it hear us speaking? How did our voices sound? Could it speak back?*

She assumed a beak as small as a chickadee's couldn't pronounce human words, but she's been wrong before.

The bird looked at her and started to make its way toward the red oak tree about 100 feet from the office's entrance, flapping its wings as Anissa slowly began to process the situation. Maybe the bird processed quicker because of its higher resting metabolism. Do higher heart rates mean the brain processes quicker? That reactions are quicker? Is that a thing?

Anissa didn't know any of this. She had wanted to be a biology major in college, but settled on getting her bartending license instead. A more reliable career path. She supposed she could look it up when she got back to her desk.

Not now. Now was not the time to think about that. Now, she had to focus.

She watched the bird fly toward the red oak tree. She followed.

She watched the bird fly up, look at her, then swoop down to fly up again.

"Oh, no. No, no, no," Anissa muttered. "I'm not climbing that."

It looked down at her again, expectantly. She assumed if it could, it would have rolled its eyes at her. Those were the vibrations it was giving her. Disappointment.

"No—it's not that I don't want to. It's that I can't!" She tried to think of a way to motion this. She held her side, as if she were being stabbed. "I'm hurt," she said slowly, as if this would help the bird understand better.

She thought back on movies where smaller animals hear human voices as slowed down and deep already. Was slowing down her voice making her even less comprehensible?

The bird didn't care about her injury. It pecked at its nest, which held a notebook. When the chickadee tried to lift the notebook, it came up short. All she heard was a slip from when the cover slipped out of its beak, then a tiny *thud* when it landed back into its grass and twig padding.

"How did you get that up there in the first place?" Anissa asked, more to herself than to the bird. She realized she wasn't going to get a response, but it wasn't quite a rhetorical question, either. If it were at all possible, she would have welcomed a response.

The bird didn't respond. Instead, it kept motioning for her to go up the tree, to climb the tree. It then changed its strategy—landing on branches that were easily reachable to her, as if to try to show her where to start.

Anissa looked around.

I mean, she was curious to see what was in that notebook. Was she willing to hurt herself more for it?

Fuck it.

She reached for the first branch and pulled herself up. She tried to favor one side, pulling more on her right than her left, but she still felt a sharp pain whenever she exerted her left side at all. She tried to correct as she moved, working with the pain as her aspirin continued to wear off.

Once she was up on the first branch, the chickadee landed on the second branch, landing directly in front of her face. The two looked at each other, eye to eye, and Anissa noticed how distinctly focused it seemed to be. More human than bird.

What the actual fuck is going on?

She moved to the next branch, the pain intensifying. Would she be able to jump from the tree once she was done? Would that do more damage? She wasn't sure if she'd be able to make it down on her own, and she didn't want to get caught up in the tree.

The bird continued to the next branch. Flying up then down again, as if it were a coach cheering her on through the final stretch of a marathon.

But as she reached for the next branch, she felt a new, stinging pain on her torso, near the previous fractures—but on a much higher level.

"FUCK!" she shouted as she fell, the pain catching her by surprise and off balance until she dropped to the ground. She passed out immediately.

Chapter 20

When she awoke, Anissa was surrounded by a small, blurred crowd who she recognized vaguely, but not by name. People she had seen come in and out of the office.

"She's waking up," a woman said, wearing a red blouse with its sleeves rolled up. It was Susan from New Beginnings—but this is the first time she and Anissa met, as Susan usually ignored her when she would walk in with her iced latte each morning.

"SHE'S WAKING UP!" Susan shouted to a growing crowd who had gathered around Anissa, surrounding her on, thankfully, the grass she landed on. *Thank Christ it hadn't been the concrete sidewalk, by some sort of miracle,* she thought to herself before the pain set in again. As if by reaching she further injured her ribs, somehow, strained an already damaged muscle trying to reach to the next branch.

Either way, the pain was excruciating.

From the heightened sound of gasps and chatter, Anissa figured there were probably 20—25 people surrounding her now.

How embarrassing. How completely embarrassing. This would be the second time she fell out of a tree in public. Another time that this could possibly make the news.

Fuck. Not again. Anissa sighed.

"Is there any blood? Do we need a paramedic?" someone from her left shouted.

Anissa waited for them to answer before she looked for herself. But if they were asking if there was any blood versus simply seeing it, perhaps that was a good sign. At least she wasn't bleeding out externally.

She tried turning toward them, but her side. Her side was shooting pain. She lifted her arms, and she could. She wiggled her toes, and she could. *All good signs.* It felt like her side was in worse shape, but at least it was centralized.

But when she tried to get up, she felt her back.

Not broken or fractured, just sore.

"The blood is coming out the back of her head! Blood coming from her head! Someone get a bandage or some cloth!" Susan shouted again. Instead of helping Anissa up, she stood in front of her waving her hands, as if to say *I don't know what to do here I don't know what to do here someone else take control,* yet she refused to relinquish control.

Anissa couldn't tell if Susan had any first-aid training or knew any best practices, or if she was just a concerned citizen who decided to step in. From what Anissa was gathering, chances that she was certified in anything were *probably not* to *definitely not.*

Anissa sat herself up as someone tore a T-shirt they had stored in the back of their car to make a makeshift headwrap for her.

"You've got to sanitize it first, you asshole," Anissa heard from somewhere behind her, but the words sounded warped, stretched, deep—as if they were made of taffy that was getting harder and slower as they continued to stretch out.

She turned to look, but she couldn't turn all the way. But what she did see?

Dennis.

Dennis was in the driver's seat of his Buick, watching from the parking lot.

Why?

"I did just wash it yesterday. It was going to be my gym shirt for tonight." The taffy-like words continued as she tried to connect why Dennis was just, well, sitting there. Staring.

His eyes.

It was his eyes.

And even though Anissa couldn't see them—not only was he wearing sunglasses and he was too far away—but she could sense them. He was staring right at her.

Eating what appeared to be a large sandwich.

But that seemed like an act—secondary to keeping an eye on her.

And while this didn't seem abnormal if it had been anyone else, there was something about the way he was positioned. The way he was parked. Too good of a view. Too easy to watch without doing anything.

"No, I mean you should sanitize the wound, you idiot. I'd hope the shirt is clean," the words started leveling as Anissa returned to the immediate.

"How are you doing, honey? You coming to?" Susan said, sweet but thin, like sugar water.

"I'm fine, I think. I think I'm fine. How long have I been here?" Anissa looked to the sun. It couldn't have been that long. It hadn't moved too far in the sky. Maybe 20 minutes, tops, but that could mean something. That could have a lasting effect.

"I don't know—I was just walking in and I saw you here, you know? You shouldn't be climbing trees on your lunch breaks, especially not trees like this. You have got to be more careful!"

Anissa nodded, noting how ridiculous she must look right now. How in the hell would she ever explain to anyone that she was just following a chickadee that lured her to the top of a tree?

Was the chickadee trying to kill her?

She couldn't tell. It was gone, now. It probably flew away quickly after she fell. Not that it could do much to help her, being as small as it was, but that still seemed cold, somehow. As if the chickadee leaving her to die was a personal insult.

"You should thank that man over there for finding you. Dennis. When I walked by, he was helping you out, you know that, right? Once you get mended up and are feeling better, you really should thank Dennis, okay?" said the man who had given her his shirt.

She looked back to Dennis's car, which was now creeping away, slowly but deliberately.

"I'll be fine," Anissa said as she motioned for everyone to back up, to give her space. She tried to push herself up, but a jolt of pain shot down her left side, no matter which side she favored.

She'd have to sit here until they all left if she didn't want them to worry about her, which she knew wouldn't happen. They wouldn't leave until she got up, but she wanted them to leave so she *could* get up.

A true conundrum.

"You've just fallen from a tree," Susan said, more so for the crowd than for Anissa. As if she were doing a call and response, where she'd say, "You've just fallen from a tree" and the rest of the crowd would say, "Yeah!"

"Please, I'd rather not air my business."

"But if it's on company property, it's *our* business to make sure you're okay, isn't that right?" Again, Susan said this more for the audience than to reassure. Anissa had never felt in less capable hands than this showboat, who was pretending as if the situation was under control with her at the helm.

"I'm fine, but I need a bit of air. I'll get up in a second," Anissa tried it, though she knew it wouldn't work.

"Let me help you." Susan stretched her freshly manicured hand out to help her up, looking over her shoulder to see if anyone was watching.

They were. They all were. Susan smiled.

Anissa did not. Instead, she propelled herself up by sheer pride-driven force and started walking toward the front entrance. Slowly. She tried to hide the limp and the new aches she found as she started to move her body again. Her wrist was hurt, possibly twisted. Her elbow, scraped. She was bleeding from the back of her head, but nothing drastic. It was wrapped up. She would be fine. The true hero of this story—the unspoken one who simply wrapped her head, no acknowledgment.

"Do you need any more—"

“No, I’m fine,” Anissa said without turning around, walking as quickly as she could to get out of there, out of sight, so she could process what had just happened.

What just happened?

She turned on her phone to text her friend, Steph, but decided against it. What would she say?

“Hey, so I fell out of a tree because a chickadee wanted to show me a notebook.”

What the fuck? That’s the only proper response to that text.

Maybe these injuries would mingle with the sea of other injuries she’s sustained in the past week. Maybe they wouldn't even notice when they picked her up today. Maybe it’d be fine, and everything would blow over.

It had never been that way before—somehow, the word always got out. But maybe this time would be different. *Maybe.*

Chapter 21

Derrick had gone with Ericka when Anissa's MSN came out of the register only a few moments before, when she had fallen out of the tree.

They ran down to the basement as soon as Ericka got the email. This time, she was sure to knock on Derrick's door, to make sure he felt included—to make sure he didn't start to get suspicious.

Suspicious of what? Ericka wasn't sure. He already knew everything. It's not like she was hiding anything from him, except perhaps the manufactured urgency.

"Hey, one just came in. Let's hurry up, yeah?" She nearly choked on the words. She felt so stupid still doing this, every time, knowing that in most cases, it didn't really matter if the soul was processed right away or not. The soul could hang out for a little while before getting recycled. Perfectly natural—so long as it didn't become a habit.

On the seventh floor, they navigated past Jared the janitor, who was mopping up what looked to be either an unfortunate bodily catastrophe or leftover chili.

No, it was chili.

They both smiled and nodded at each other when they both realized it was chili, though their smiles were thin. They were transparently inauthentic, like a face tick to an uncomfortable catalyst.

Sixth floor.

Fifth floor.

On the fourth floor, there was a woman neither of them recognized who was sprinting up and down the stairs. When they came around the corner, she looked genuinely embarrassed, as if this was the first time anyone had seen her do this—and now, her cover was blown.

"Oh wow, I didn't see you there—"

"No worries," Ericka said, without skipping a beat.

Third floor.

Second floor.

First floor.

Basement.

Beep, beep, beep, beep, click.

The door swung open, and Ericka held up the receipt tape.

"Oh, no. I know this one. No. This one is one we ignore."

"What? But you didn't even check," Derrick said.

"I see this one all the time. Trust me. We don't process this one."

Derrick looked at the number, as if he might remember. He didn't. After he looked at it, he wasn't entirely sure why. It wouldn't lend any answers.

"Can you show me?"

"Sure, but you have to promise me this will not affect your day. I know this might start to feel a little personal, but you have to—"

"You have to learn how to separate it," Derrick said. "I'm sorry, I shouldn't have interrupted you. Dennis said that same thing to me earlier. He said it would start to get difficult."

She pursed her lips and nodded, in that tight-lipped smile people do when they're uncomfortable and can't find the right words.

"Well, for once, he's not wrong," she said when she finally found the words.

"It's Anissa, isn't it?"

Ericka paused before proceeding, shifting her weight. "You have to promise not to tell," she said as she shoved the receipt in her back pocket. "I know that's a lot to ask, but I'm hoping it won't be a problem and it won't come up again while you're here."

"I don't understand. Did she almost die? Is she hurt?"

"Most likely on both." Ericka paused, understanding what she was saying. The question wasn't about the logistics. It was about emotions—*is my friend okay?*—to which she answered *no, most likely not.*

"I know it's not the most comfortable thing to think about. I understand that. I know. I can only imagine what you're feeling."

"I just don't understand the end game. Why do we do this? Where does the list come from?" He couldn't hide the emotion from his voice anymore. The dam broke.

"I don't know why Anissa is on the list, if that's what you mean." Ericka paused, startled but not surprised by his sudden emotional shift. "The only thing I know is we are not allowed to let her die."

Ericka had a vague understanding of why the list existed. Something had happened with those souls—either they were growing immune to the recycling process, refusing to give up their memories, or someone had tampered with them to make it so. This list was their best solution until they came up with an actual solution. This list was Death, Inc.'s best idea for a temporary fix until they found a true lasting remedy.

This isn't what Derrick wanted to hear, though. The hypotheses. If she couldn't give him any conclusive answers, she knew it was best to feign ignorance in this case.

"But she just keeps getting hurt. She's just going to keep getting hurt. What if it gets more serious and she ends up in a coma?"

"In all honesty, Derrick, we don't know how the death took place under normal circumstances. All we do is we process here."

"But you know her—you know she's hurt. She can't keep getting injured in the state she's—"

"You don't think I know that?" Ericka now surprised herself when her voice raised, when emotion lifted in her chest and pushed out her thoughts, unfiltered.

She caught herself, composed herself, then continued.

"What I'm saying is I know it's hard. It's incredibly difficult, especially when you recognize someone. Or, in your case, when you recognize someone, but that only means they'll continue suffering." Ericka knew this firsthand, but it didn't feel right to address it here. She didn't want it to look like she was trying to one-up him, as if she were mitigating his experience, as if she were saying *if I can get through it, you can, too.* She knew that was not how grief worked, and sometimes, camaraderie in grief is not the best solution. Sometimes, the griever, no matter which stage they're in, just needs to get it out.

"Why can't we just pass them on, though? I don't understand."

"If I had that answer, I would tell you. I swear. I would let you know. But I don't know. I don't know anything about the folder, or what would happen if we passed them on."

She paused as if assessing how to proceed. "But I'm not willing to risk finding out that maybe my assessment is wrong, that maybe I don't have all the facts and I've killed someone who wasn't supposed to die. I'm not in this business to kill a future Maya Angelou, or someone of equal influence."

"I understand," Derrick said, but his tone gave him away. While he understood, it was clear he did not agree.

"I know it's probably hard for you to grapple with this, so I'd understand if you don't want to be a part of this process anymore, if that makes it easier."

Derrick paused. In his head, his thoughts were churning. He tried to make his face blank, but in his head, he thought he figured it out.

He thought.

He thought there was a way to fix this, a simple way, a collaborative way. But now? He wasn't sure.

He had to figure it out for himself.

He had an idea.

“No, that’s fine,” Derrick said, trying to sound as casual and sincere as he could, given the circumstances. “I’ll let you know if it becomes a problem.”

“Okay, that sounds good. Please do, and know it won’t be a problem if it *does* become a problem. I get it.” Ericka paused, wrung her hands, then clapped them together, as if to signify a tone shift. As if to reset the entire past five minutes. “Well, let’s get back to it, yeah? I’m sure you have a lot to go over.”

As before, the ascent is always more uncomfortable than the descent, where there is no immediate destination—there is no urgency.

They didn’t have anything to talk about, and neither knew what to say. Each footprint seemed to echo louder than the last. They got to the fourth floor to see the woman who had been sprinting up and down the stairs was still not done, and she still looked equally embarrassed when they came across her again. They got to the seventh floor to see the chili that had been spilled was now cleaned up, though the stench still hung in the air. They both smiled at each other when they passed each of the floor milestones, to acknowledge them. They didn’t say anything past a smile and a nod.

“Let me know if you need anything,” Ericka said so abruptly that she startled Derrick as soon as they left the stairwell.

“Sure!” he said mid-jump, quickly. The hair on his arms stuck straight up.

***

When Derrick got back to his desk, he noticed he had another email from Anissa.

This time, urgent.

Fuck.

He had to regroup with Dennis.

That was what he had to do next.

When Derrick got anxious, the world seemed like one giant slur of responsibilities. Ones that were all equally urgent and equally vying for his time. *Check Anissa's emails and respond*, *group with Dennis*, and *write these articles* lived in his head as giant cartoon-like exclamation points. Each would be equally catastrophic and devastating if he ignored any of them, or if he prioritized one over the other.

He had to breathe. *Breathe.*

Except in this case, everything was actually catastrophic and devastating. Everything fell on everything else—a domino effect. If he chose one thing, there would be horrific repercussions for the other. There was no easy or clear way out.

He basically had to choose who he wanted to align with and who he would fuck over.

Or kill, in the case of Anissa.

But it wasn't really killing her, he justified in his head. She was already on her way out. Right now, they were simply saving her by ignoring her when she came through the system. They were not actively saving her. But the absence of action, in this case, should never warrant praise.

Or should it?

These thoughts crowded his head because he had already made up his mind, in part. Not completely—the pendulum was still swinging, but it was starting to favor one side. He could not ignore that favoring.

In every instance, he would be killing something—it would be his job, someone else's career, or someone. And while on its face one seemed much more extreme, it was the situation that put everything on equal ground, at least in Derrick's mind. The equal inevitability of each.

He cradled his head in his palms, with his elbows on the desk. His back was arched over in utter defeat, as if he made himself smaller to hide from all consequences entirely. He wished to be Gregor Samsa—he would *kill* to wake up one day as a giant bug, one devoid of these responsibilities, one that could survive simply by crawling under a rock and living out the rest of its days. What a perfect life.

But he couldn't do that today. There was absolutely no chance that Kafka was his psychic today, or was predicting Derrick's specific future in *Metamorphosis*.

Today, Derrick had to focus on reality. On breathing. Breathe in, breathe out. Just like he had seen on so many YouTube videos he used to watch in college—the only thing that relaxed him when he was in what he assumed was the hardest chapter of his life. The focus was to connect on his breathing—breathe in for 10 seconds, breathe out for 10 seconds. Breathing in through the nose and out through the mouth. Alternate nostril breathing, where you inhale through your left nostril and exhale from your right (otherwise known as Nadi Shodhana, the pranayama yoga practice this originated from).

In college, he tried to breathe out the bad vibes of his classmates, their perceived judgment, or the impending test that was coming up that he couldn't focus enough to study on. What he was trying to breathe in was wealth, social prosperity, serenity. If only it were that easy.

If only he knew better.

He tried to channel those videos, regardless.

Breathe in. On making the right move. *Breathe out.* On making sure he wasn't being impulsive and reactive. *Breathe in.* On not killing your new friend or acquaintance or whatever she was to him. *Breathe out.* On maybe, it's not so much killing as it is saving her, whoever she was to him—the hardship. *Breathe in.* The pain. Wait, was he breathing in pain? *Breathe out.*

He tried to wait to make sure he wouldn't run into Anissa at the end of the day.

5:30 pm.

He knew she got a ride from her roommates, and he assumed (as long as nothing terrible or catastrophic had happened to her and she wasn't currently in the hospital) that it would be the same today. That they would pick her up and she would go home right around 5:00 pm.

Unless they were late.

They were late. If he were to ask Anissa, he'd find out that Gary had to pick up their dog, Stacy, from the vet earlier that afternoon and there were some complications, so he was getting the back seat of his car cleaned out before he picked her up. Not a big deal, and Anissa was grateful for the wait.

As much as Derrick was trying to avoid her, she was trying to confront him.

Two emails, missed. There's no way. There's no way he missed both of those unless he was actively avoiding her.

Why would he be avoiding her unless he was hiding something?

But if there was a chance, she was going to give him the benefit of the doubt.

She couldn't go home without knowing.

Two emails. The second, sent with high importance. Both contained the same sentence—"What do you know about the chickadee?"

He clearly either he wasn't checking his email, or he didn't want to talk about the chickadee.

Her gut said the latter, but she had to find out.

As Derrick entered the lobby, he saw the back of Anissa's head. It was covered in some sort of makeshift bandage made from a black Nike shirt. The swoop was plastered across her head as if she was a living endorsement—a billboard of sorts, as to say, "Just Do It—and here's what will happen if you do."

His plan was to walk quickly, so maybe she wouldn't see him. Maybe if he hurried, she would only catch his back and wouldn't register that he was who he was.

But that didn't happen. That's never how it happens.

"Derrick, what do you know about the chickadee?" Anissa shouted at his back as he quickened his pace. She would have stood, but she was stuck in her chair. Even the shout pained her, her vocal cords powered by pure adrenaline.

Derrick heard her doubling over with an *agh* and *gah*—a pain so strong he could feel it in his own gut—but he didn't turn around. As much as his instinct told him to help her, he knew he couldn't. Kind of like how every wildlife specialist tells you not to help injured wildlife unless it is absolutely necessary, to not destroy the natural order.

But this was his friend. Or at least an acquaintance. Was that an insensitive comparison to make to about a human, whether they were friends or acquaintances?

He had never stopped to pause on whether they were truly friends, or if she was just the first person to acknowledge him as a human being at this job. Was this his mind distancing himself, the way pack animals distance themselves from those who get sick?

I have got to turn off the Nat Geo, he thought to himself.

"Sorry, I can't talk now," Derrick said, the door shutting abruptly behind him. He said this before he let the actual message behind his thoughts sink in—the one questioning how it was okay to let this woman die.

He knew she wouldn't be able to go after him, to question him. He'd have time to get to his car before she even got herself out of her seat. Could she even open the door?

He tried to block his thoughts out as he walked toward his Honda Civic, at the far end of the lot. He tried to unlock the driver's-side door, but the lock was stuck. Tried it again. Stuck again. Tried again—this time, a *click*. He opened the door and grabbed his Ray-Ban knockoffs from the seat before sitting on them. He reminded himself to put them away next time before going to work. He thought about Anissa again, but tried to block it out as he put the key in the ignition.

The CD he listened to on the way to work was playing *Pet Sounds* by the Beach Boys, which no longer seemed fitting. Silence seemed like the best soundtrack, now.

He paused the CD and put forth every effort to shove every thought out of his brain. *Breathe in, breathe out.* No thoughts, just breathing.

Chapter 22

When Derrick got in the next day, Dennis was already in his office. Not his own office, but Derrick's. Not sitting in the chair across from the desk, but sitting in Derrick's chair—feet propped up on the desk, arms tightly crossed across his chest. He swiveled in Derrick's office chair until he faced him straight on, to acknowledge him.

"So . . . what happened yesterday?" Dennis said before Derrick could say a word.

Derrick opened his mouth to speak. "I—"

"It's just there was supposed to be a soul passed on, and I couldn't help but notice that very soul is checking people into our office today. Currently."

Derrick fumbled for words. Dennis continued.

"Rather painfully, at that. I'm shocked she didn't take a day. Have you seen the back of her head? I know she tried to cover it with a ponytail, but Christ, that bandage? Still bloody? Brutal. And I guess they're right when they say it's hard to wash blood out of hair. Looking a bit auburn today, isn't she?"

"I can explain," Derrick said before he could stop himself. *But could he? Was he allowed to?* And as much as his heart was racing, this felt like, in part, a relief. If he could just say it, that would be one decision made. One concrete decision made. He'd just have to—

"Well, then, go ahead. Shoot. Tell me what's going on, Derrick."

Derrick paused.

This was it. He had made his decision. He was going to tell Dennis what was happening, and hope things laid in place from there.

But that meant he had to spit the words out. He had to be an active participant in a moral grey area, one that would have catastrophic circumstances for people he grew to know.

Even though he has only been here for a week. *Christ, one week.*

Dennis continued. "At least to the best of your understanding. I realize you've only been here for, what, a week, now? Wow. Holy shit, this has been chaos for you."

Derrick nodded. *TGIF. Thank God it's Friday.* Something in his gut told him that would have been embarrassing to say out loud, so he kept it to himself.

"Just tell me what happened in that room, and let me know if anything looked off compared to the other times you've been in there. Even if you don't fully understand it. That's cool. I totally get that. But did anything seem off, and did anyone tell you to keep quiet on it?"

"It's the folders."

The words slid out from Derrick's lips, like a toddler who just realized their fork contained too much spaghetti and marinara after they shoved a heaping forkful in their mouth. A waterfall of words.

Dennis paused and shook his head, as if Derrick was saying something he was already intimately familiar with—dismissive, while still acknowledging. "Yes, the folders. There are three of them."

Derrick hurriedly said, "The fourth. It's in the fourth."

"Wait, what's in the fourth? A *fourth* folder?" Dennis sat up, and took his feet off the desk, elbows resting there instead. Dennis was thinking it would be a misstep on something he already knew. He did not expect an entire process to be kept from him, and formally. Or at least formal enough to have a folder designated to it.

"That's where we have the other list," Derrick said.

Dennis exhaled. "Christ, could you just tell me what you mean in one succinct sentence instead of making me pull it out of you? I get this is hard for you, and I totally get that. I can relate. But save us the time—"

"That's the list of people we can't kill."

"Excuse me?"

"That's the list of people—"

"I heard you the first time. I was saying that more as an exclamation."

"Sorry."

"No, no. No. I get it. This is weird. Whew! This is weird for me. Here I am thinking I'm not the office bitch—turns out, I've been the fool this entire time."

Derrick didn't know what to say. I guess that's how this could come off, right? In that Dennis just wouldn't notice or wouldn't care if the soul didn't come back to be recycled? Derrick nodded, but as a way to hang his head—to adjust his posture to try to acclimate.

"Was it Harold or Ericka who told you about the folder?"

"Both, actually."

"Well, shit," Dennis put his head in his hands and rubbed his face. He laughed in one staccato laugh, one incredulous burst. "Can you gauge this for me? Does it seem established? How big is the list?"

"Not too big. Maybe a full page."

"You realize Schuester has, what, like 200 people?"

"Schuester's more like a few thousand, and the list is actually a national—"

"Now's not the time for details, Derrick."

"Right, right. Sorry." Derrick ran his hands through his hair not because he needed to fix it, but because he needed to do something. Anything. He couldn't just stand there. His anxiety would make him explode if he stayed still. Shatter. Crumble. And while that sounds like all those things can't happen at once, then congratulations—it sounds like you most likely don't suffer from an anxiety disorder. That flight-or-fight feeling is strange when there is nowhere you can go, when the conflict you're trying to run away from is an idea or an abstraction rather than a physical predator.

"Well, does it seem like something they've been doing for a while, or is it something they scrounged up recently?"

"I would say established, but—"

"For how long?"

"But I have no idea for how long." Derrick finished his thought.

"I see." Dennis got up from the chair. He leaned over the desk. Sat back down again. Looked at Derrick. "I think we should talk this over, between us. A nothing-leaves-this-room situation. Let's figure this out."

"I'm not sure if I'll be the best—"

"No, Derrick. You're the perfect person for this. I clearly can't trust Ericka or Harold on this one. You're all I've got."

"I'm just not sure how much I can do to help."

Dennis paused. Not because he was thinking about what Derrick had said, but because he was lost in his own thoughts. His own gears were spinning far too loudly to process anything from Derrick. "Can you take a picture of that folder with your phone? Or the list?"

"There's no way I can make that look natural," Derrick said, in his one moment of pure clarity in their entire interaction.

"Good point." Dennis fell back into his thoughts again. Derrick sat across, crossed his legs, uncrossed his legs, and kept a beat on the armrest.

"Could you please stop that? I'm trying to concentrate," Dennis said, motioning at Derrick's tapping fingers.

"Right, right. Sorry." Derrick's foot started to tap, as if he had to release some sort of beat, but he held his leg down with his hand. Tried his best to keep still.

"Are you in any way ready to do the process on your own? Do you think they'd trust you?"

"I'd say hard no, not at all. Ericka hasn't even let me do anything yet even if she's there—much less on my own."

"But Harold?"

"I mean, I've only seen him take care of one, but again, it's only been a week."

"Interesting. What about when Ericka is in a meeting?"

"I honestly have no idea. Like I said, I've—"

"You've only been here for a week, right. We all know that. But what does your *gut* say on how many times Harold handles that process? Can he?"

"Oh yeah, he definitely can, it's just it seems like—"

"Okay, good. Good, good," Dennis said, pausing for a moment. "We're in this together now, right? You're not going to flake out on me here, are you? You're going to help me with this? Even if it means passing your friend's soul on to the other side?"

Derrick's mind was already made up, but there was something about *saying it* that seemed so final. It was clear this was the path he was going to take. He was going to help Dennis.

But to say it out loud?

"I mean, you realize I know the secret that you were supposed to keep. I think we're stuck with each other now."

But there was one thing Derrick had to do.

"Tell me what happened to the chickadee."

"Derrick, now's not the time—"

"I need to know what I'm getting into before I proceed, so I'm going to need to know everything."

Dennis paused and ran his hand through his hair before shoving it back into his pocket. "I have to start by saying it started as consensual. It was not supposed to turn into this."

Derrick raised his brows.

Dennis continued. "It was an experiment on a willing participant, to see if I could pass a soul on without recycling it. To see if we could pass memories down from one being to the next."

"So it is actually a human soul in a chickadee's body." Derrick said the words but didn't fully process them. His brain was working as the words trickled from his mouth.

"It started off as consensual, as I said. She agreed to do it. Christine is her name, if you believe she kept her name after her memories were passed down to the next being. We wanted to see if we could pass down life experiences, and how new experiences would layer on previous iterations. But. . . well, I think you know the rest."

Derrick's unfocused eyes cast downward, lost in thought.

"It was a one-time thing for me. And because it wasn't an accident, I can assure you it won't happen again. But this Anissa thing . . ."

"This Anissa thing will keep happening," Derrick agreed.

Granted, the chickadee situation was still shocking—somehow, more shocking now that Derrick knew her name. *Christine.*

Derrick looked up at Dennis, trying to read him. "Did Christine know what she was getting into. Like, *really* know? Did you really explain it to her?"

"We talked it over for two years. There had been experiments done previously in Death, Inc.—passing souls to different animal hosts—and the chickadee was the most humane out of all their experiments. We decided based on that. I had no idea it'd turn into, well . . ."

Dennis paused before continuing. Derrick nodded as if to say *please proceed.*

Dennis continued. "She had Stage 4 breast cancer, so it was either death forever or this. Transferring her soul and her memories to a chickadee's body seemed like the obvious choice at the time," Dennis said, looking down deep in thought—lost in a memory. Then, he looked Derrick dead in the eye. "If I could take it back knowing what I know now, trust me, I would. But I can't."

This isn't what Derrick expected. He expected that, if Dennis was involved, he would brush it off like he did the red-winged blackbird, or like anything else he deemed problematically not his problem. But this was different.

"You said it was based on a series of experiments. What does that mean?" Derrick asked.

Dennis sighed, switching from his uncomfortable-vulnerable to his much more comfortable-logical state. "The soul recycling process is still fairly new, you have to remember. There's debate on how ethical our processes are, how to best proceed—it's not as cut and dry as it seems on the surface, but I'm sure you've figured that out already. I've learned the hard way that putting a human soul inside a chickadee body, even if only a temporary holding spot, is not in my moral comfort zone. There are those who disagree on that, which we can discuss later on, if you feel comfortable with that." The hurt showed in Dennis's eyes, to the point where Derrick thought he might cry. He tried to create a welcoming space for that as best he could, without forcing it.

"I believe you, by the way. When you say you'd take it back if you could. I do," Derrick said. While it felt uncomfortable to say, it still felt important enough to mention.

Dennis cleared his throat, in an attempt to move past it. "Well, now that we have that out of the way, are you with me or not?"

Derrick had one more question that felt even more uncomfortable to ask, given the emotional turn in conversation. Uncomfortable, but again, important to mention.

His bills.

"What about my job?" Derrick said, definitively as he could.

"They pay interns here?" Dennis asked. Derrick thought he was joking, but his face was serious.

"I'm not an intern."

Dennis looked at him, puzzled. He opened his phone, opened his Outlook, then clicked on Derrick's name before holding up the phone. "That's not what your employee bio says in the directory," Derrick's face turned white.

Dennis showed his phone screen to Derrick, pinching to zoom in on *Marketing Intern* below Derrick's name. "See? Death, Inc., Marketing Intern," Dennis laughed, one single dry laugh, sliding his phone back in his pocket. "Sure sounds like you're an intern to me. But if you help me out now, I can make sure you aren't an intern for long."

Derrick sighed. He hadn't gotten his first paycheck yet, but he assumed it would be coming based on all the paperwork he signed. Based on how reputable Ericka seemed. Based on, well, every job he had leading up to this.

Had I been fucked with?

"Can you promise that for sure?" Derrick asked, questioning everything.

"I can promise that with certainty," Dennis said, pausing as if he were doing the calculations in his head. "There may have to be a few loopholes and a few hoops we have to jump through, and you might have a different title than you—"

"No. No bullshit. I need to have a job if I help you out," Derrick said, looking Dennis in the eye in a way Dennis hadn't expected. Eyebrows raised.

"Let's talk logistics once we're done here, but I can promise that you will have a job—"

"A job that pays me," Derrick said, which suddenly felt like an important distinction.

"You will have a job that pays the same, if not more, once we're done here, or once you get fired. As long as you stick to the plan. You got that?"

"What's the plan?"

"Let's figure that out over lunch next week. You still okay with lunch?"

"We're going to wait until after the . . . can't we just talk about it now?"

Dennis's phone beeped. He looked at it. "No can do. Meeting time. Both of us. Chickadee stuff. Let me do the talking."

Before Derrick could answer anything, Dennis had already opened the door. Behind, was Ericka. She looked from Dennis to Derrick several times, like a spectator at a tennis match.

"Good morning, Derrick," Ericka said with a bit more precision than Derrick was used to. Knowing eyes. Derrick tried to keep himself from shrinking, tried to hold himself up with confidence—but he could feel his insides inflating.

Had he done the right thing? Was this the right thing? Was there a clear good side and bad side, something he was missing? Was it that big of a grey area?

Most importantly, and most urgently—could she know what he had just done?

Chapter 23

Ericka did not know what Derrick had just done, but whatever it was, she did not have a good feeling.

There was no reason for Derrick to be caught up in a meeting without her. There was no reason for Dennis to be talking with Derrick in private unless it was about the chickadee thing, which she highly doubted. Dennis seemed too, well . . . humbled for that.

Unless there was something she didn't know.

It wasn't that Ericka was a control freak. She just found that things ran smoother when she was at the helm, and when she was privy to everything behind the scenes. When she was left out the of the loop, that's when things began to slip.

Or at least, that's how it seemed to her.

She had never seen Dennis this unfocused.

What the fuck is going on?

No time. She didn't have time to go over this now. She'd have to figure it out later.

Yes. Later. Where all the deadlines lived. That hypothetical later.

That aside, something seemed off.

This had to be about yesterday. Anissa. *That wrapped up too cleanly with Derrick to be truly resolved,* she thought. She should have known.

That was the only thing she could think of—the only thing that could have driven this outcome.

Yet, still, she couldn't bring herself to believe it. She couldn't ask outright. It's possible something happened in his personal life. Perhaps Dennis was trying to be less of an asshole around the new hire.

They sat next to each other in the meeting. But didn't they before? Was she overthinking this?

"Ericka, *yoohoo*. Are you with us?" she heard Susan say, snapping her out of her thought train. Fuck, what had she missed?

"Yes, sorry. So sorry. I was lost in thought for a second. I'm here. Sorry," she said as she pulled out an empty notebook and a chair to sit in, next to Derrick.

"What I was saying is this can't be another newspaper article. This chickadee. We have to sort this out before we have a microphone in our face."

Oh, funny you're worried about that now. The words hung in the back of Ericka's throat, but she swallowed them just in time. Not when there's a former employee saying this company is killing people. But when a chickadee starts leaving notes outside of the office, that's when it's time to call the guards.

Christ.

"Of course," Ericka said out loud, though everything inside her was saying the opposite. This had been her world recently. Her body told her to do one thing, and she'd end up doing the other. In an attempt to do the right thing she went against her instinct. Her chest hurt from all of the pressure she put on it.

"Well, do you have any ideas?" Susan said, "If I remember correctly, that's where we left off, correct? With you investigating what was going on with this chickadee thing?"

"I think the plan was we were both going to—"

"No. No that wasn't the plan. Right, Denise? That wasn't the plan?" Susan looked at her assistant, Denise, who nodded in agreement. Thoughtlessly definitive, as always.

Of course.

Ericka turned to Derrick and Dennis, who were sitting quietly at the end of the table. Unlike Dennis's promise only five minutes before, he did none of the talking. Nothing. Not a peep. What he did do—he shrugged. As if to say, "Who's to say what happened?"

Susan said, "We're not looking for exact answers. We realize it hasn't been that long since we last met, and I'm guessing you've had a lot of work to do since we've last spoken." When she looked at them after she was done speaking, it was difficult to tell if she was being serious or not. If she was being facetious.

Is she fucking with me? Is she implying I'm stupid? Ericka honestly couldn't tell. She was trying to check herself as she usually thought people were fucking with her, assuming she was stupid, as she often felt as a woman in any corporate setting—but this time?

"We don't have a lot of follow-up quite yet, as we are still investigating."

Susan sighed, as if she knew this would happen. As if the inevitable had happened, despite all of her best efforts and hard work. She set down her papers, looked at Ericka, then said, "Let's put a timetable on this, yeah?" Susan said as if she were talking with a kindergartener. This was not beyond Ericka. She was being demeaned. But sometimes, she was willing to take it to avoid the hassle.

This was one of those times. *Fuck it.*

"Let's reconvene in two weeks and see where we're at, then."

"Sure thing," Dennis said with a *thumbs up*, finally saying something, yet tone still distant. Derrick looked at him. Was this his definition of saying something?

Is he fucking with me, too? Ericka thought as she looked to Dennis.

They caught each other's eyes, and she saw no maliciousness. Perhaps she was overreacting. Perhaps she had too much coffee this morning and was thinking the worst of everyone.

But something seemed off. The air. The way people were dancing around their words, avoiding any direct statements. The way Dennis, well, *was,* for Christ's sake.

He never does this. They had been working together for five years, now. She had never seen him like this.

Before she could mentally return to the meeting, everyone was already packing up. Ericka heard, "Let's give everyone back 25 minutes—I'm sure we could all use it." But it wasn't in the immediate. It was muffled, shuffled behind the dialogue inside her head. She nodded just the same but kept to herself. She gathered her things, smiled to agree, then went back to her office—shaken.

***

Anissa, meanwhile, was downstairs in the lobby with a full wrap around her head.

Super sexy, she thought to herself, as the top of her vision was cut off by cotton. Her hair was in a high ponytail, but she could feel the top of her bloodied hair tangling and knotting underneath. She turned in her seat, trying to use her feet to turn rather than her battered torso. She breathed in, felt a knot of pain, then breathed out.

As much as she tried to play off that she didn't give a shit about what she looked like, this was an embarrassment. She used to wear scars as a badge of honor—as little ticks in her skin that showed she had done something and had paid her dues, but that was before these bouts started. Before the news articles started.

Now, she felt like they were making her stand out even more than she was before, if that was even possible.

She currently had two reporters in her voicemail, and her fall hadn't even been that dramatic. Pretty average, compared to some of her other injuries.

But right now, she couldn't focus on that. She had more important things to think about.

The chickadee. Why was Dennis watching? How had he helped, and why had he left? Most importantly, why does this shit *always* happen to her?

There had to be something she was missing.

She looked up Death, Inc. again.

"DEATH, INC. EUTHANIZES PEOPLE."

She had seen before. Seemed a bit off. *The Schuester Stories* had once been a reliable way to get the news, but with the rest of the page decorated with headlines like "One-Eyed Man Regenerates His Own Eye" and "Woman Claims to Have Married Bigfoot" in its archive, it was hard to take them seriously.

Anissa skimmed a few lines. She read, "Suite 6 . . ." until she reached the line, "Their salaries are paid to pass our souls onward."

She thought back on the mysterious tone around her interview—the voicemail saying they found her resume on ZipRecruiter, though she couldn't remember if she even had a resume, much less if she posted it on ZipRecruiter. Were they orchestrating all of this, somehow? Was her getting this job the final step in whatever they had planned next?

This would make sense if the accidents started happening after she started working here, but they started happening before. *Years* before.

She had to talk with Derrick. That was her only chance at understanding what the fuck was going on.

Email. That was her only lifeline. Under normal circumstances, she would just go up there, knock on his door, and demand to know what was happening—but she was not living under normal circumstances. She had to be more resourceful. More tactful. She had to use her energy wisely, and she had to be careful to not fuck it all up.

Derrick:

Sorry to email spam you ☺.

She looked at it again. Did that look too needy? Was she coming off as creepy or desperate?

She backspaced.

Derrick:

Long time no see ☺ Sorry for all the messages.

No. What if the humor didn't translate and he thought she didn't remember seeing him yesterday?

She looked at it, and read it out loud in her head. That would have to do. This way, she'd have the weekend to think it over and gather her thoughts. Run it by her roommates, Gary and Stephanie, if they didn't think she was absolutely batshit crazy. She had to keep in mind that she did just hit her head. It was hard to hide the fact that she hit her head. And, perhaps, maybe she was losing it.

But maybe this was worth pursuing.

What was happening to her was unquestionably questionable.

She hoped he opened this one—even better, responded. If he was hiding something, she told herself, he would not respond. If he wasn't, he would respond.

It's now or never.

Derrick,

Still on for Monday?

Chapter 24

"Come on, Derrick, there's another one coming through," Ericka said through Derrick's open door, just as Anissa's email came in. Impeccable timing.

"Funny, I'm not getting those emails," Derrick said, checking his inbox again.

"Oh. Huh. I didn't know that." But she did. She just didn't want to explain that she didn't trust him quite yet. Especially not now, with all of his interactions with Dennis.

"I'll look into it," Ericka said, her face contorting slightly to suppress a wink, one she decided against at the last minute. It seemed uncharacteristic, however natural the urge appeared within the muscles in her face.

Eight floors, as always. The descent was hurried. For the first time Derrick could remember, they passed no one. There was always someone in the hallway, but perhaps it was the time of day. He didn't remember going down at this time of day before—10:00 am.

But around the fourth floor, Ericka paused and looked back at Derrick.

"So. . . what were you and Dennis talking about this morning? I saw him in your office this morning. What's up?"

"Oh, you know, the usual."

"No, I don't." *Cool it, Ericka,* she thought to herself. She recalibrated her tone. "I'm just curious what business looks like on your side, and on Dennis's side. I don't get to see that side all that often." That was true. Ericka found that the best lies were always masked in some sort of truth—that way, they could be more easily remembered later. If they had that one memorable nugget of truth.

"We were just talking about the chickadee thing, but we didn't really get anywhere with it," Derrick said. He tried to sound cool, but said it too quickly.

"I see. Any progress with that, yet?" Ericka knew he was lying to her, and she wondered if he knew she was lying to him, too. *Perhaps he knows I'm suspicious*, she thought, noting to cool it and be a bit more careful.

As she entered the door code, she noticed that Derrick was standing closer than he usually would, as if he were trying to look over her shoulder. She tried to cover it with her hand as casually as she could, noting that each number had a different sounding *beep*—and noting how much of a security hazard that was in general for a locked door, but hoping he wasn't taking close notes on the sounds.

"Hopefully this will be a quick one, yeah? Always sad when you sit down to think about it, that someone in our town just died—but I guess it must be done at some point," Ericka said as she walked toward the machine spitting out the receipt. This time, a human. She referenced the first folder and found the name. Referenced the second folder.

"Do you mind if I take over on the next one?" Derrick said as Ericka ran her finger down the second folder's list. She didn't turn to look at him, but she raised her eyebrow. "It's just . . . I think I'd learn better if I did it myself. I think it'd really help me if I really got to know the process."

Ericka paused to choose her words carefully. She didn't want to scare him away.

"Let's take it slow, yeah? It might be deceiving because it is such a quick process, but it's a vital one. One misstep can be, well—you know what's happening with that chickadee. I think. Honestly, between you and me, who knows what's going on with that."

She shook her head, then refocused her attention to the list until she found what she was looking for. "Oh, Jaron Lewis. The mailman. I hope he went quick—he was such a nice guy," Ericka said with legitimate weight in her voice. He had been one of the first people to be nice to her once she moved, always remembering her name and what junk mail she despised the most.

"Is he on the list?" Derrick asked. Ericka looked at him blankly, so he elaborated. " You know, the *list*?"

"Oh, no. I would have recognized his name on there. I know he's not on the list."

She entered the number into the second machine and got the Soul Signifying Number. Grabbed the receipt. Stapled it to the paper in the third folder. *Out* folder.

"It's never easy when it's someone you know. I get that," she said, trying to clear the air. Something seemed tense, but she wasn't sure if she was imagining things.

Derrick didn't respond—not as a statement, but because he didn't have anything to say.

Ericka sighed. "Listen, if you want to talk about Anissa, know that my door is always open. I know it will probably not be an easy process, and I'm not sure of your relationship with her, but do know that my door is open."

She thought back to her time in Minneapolis, where she had to leave because of a similar instance. A man named Nathan. He had been in business school at the time, hoping to be a business strategy consultant. On three different occasions, she watched him fall down a cliff, get into a motorcycle accident, and fall through a thick plate-glass window—it was to the point where she didn't feel safe going anywhere with him anymore in case the fates would take her out to catch his fall. She did not let Nathan pass on, wondering if that was the correct way to go. It felt like the only way to go at the time. She didn't question it then.

She shook herself from her flashback. "I'm very familiar with how difficult this can be, so if you need to talk, I'm here."

She did not let Nathan pass on, wondering now if that was the correct way to go. It felt like the only way to go at the time. She didn't question it then. But now?

"Oh, no. I'm fine. Just not much to say, is all. I'm not mad about anything," Derrick said, then immediately caught the suspicious tone still lingering in his throat. "I'm being sincere when I say that. I will let you know if the Anissa stuff gets to be too much to handle. I hear you when you say that. I do." He paused, then added one more "I do," for emphasis.

It seemed to help.

But there was still something he was hiding. That was clear. Ericka could see it on his face—the way he was making too much eye contact, his visible interest yet lack of questions. In Ericka's gut she knew that something was happening, and she feared it had something to do with the fourth folder—the one she explicitly told Derrick to keep from Dennis.

But she couldn't say for certain. It was still too early to tell.

But that didn't mean she wasn't going to keep an eye on it. She made a mental note. "Well, right. Back to the office. Do you need help with anything today, or do you have any questions?"

"No, just that article I need to write for Harold."

"How is that going?"

"Great. It's going great. I think I'll have something to show both of you soon." Again, too much eye contact. He's still lying.

"That's so great to hear! I'm glad to hear it. I think Harold will be very happy." She tried to communicate that she caught his bluff with her eyes, but it didn't seem to register. Closed off. He seemed closed off, as if he were waiting for the conversation to be done until he could take a breath.

She walked toward the door, toward the stairwell.

Maybe he was planning on quitting? He was just saying what they wanted to hear until he found something better?

She went over the possible telltale signs as she ascended the first and second floors, then scratched that idea.

But that wouldn't explain the interest. The looking over her shoulder. The . . . well . . . the feeling that something just wasn't right. All of it.

For the next six floors, she thought over what that could be. How she could figure it out? Did she want to figure it out? How quickly would she have to figure it out before it meant bad news for her?

Anissa. That would be her key—unless Anissa had something to do with it, which Ericka had a distinct feeling that she did not. The way she acted after her fall the other day—even if what Ericka heard was secondhand—showed that Anissa had no idea what was happening to her. So she had no idea about what they did, any sort of list, or that she was on one.

Anissa. She would have to talk with Anissa. Somehow.

Chapter 25

Anissa saw a message appear in her inbox from Ericka, an employee with a Death, Inc. email address. Not just an email, but an email invite.

Two hours from now. Two hours from now, she'd at least have some answers. She hoped.

She clicked **Accept Invite.**

Fuck, she thought as she unknowingly turned in a direction that cut into her side, again.

This has got to stop.

Make it stop.

Someone make it stop.

***

"Thank you for meeting with me, Anissa," Ericka said, still unsure of what her agenda was. She crossed her hands, bending and twisting her thumbs together before she noticed it and stopped. *Just play it cool*, she thought to herself, but the moment you try to act cool is the moment you are 100% not cool. A scientific fact.

"No problem," Anissa said, short. She wasn't sure if hiding her pain was the right move, but it seemed right.

Until she remembered the bandage on her head. Not exactly subtle. On top of it, she itched, subconsciously, and the bandage shifted—even more uncomfortably, if that was possible. As soon as she noticed, she said *oh, God* under her breath and set her hands mindfully in her lap, with purpose, as if to say *I'm not going to touch that again, don't worry.*

Ericka nodded, trying not to notice. "Sounds like you had quite the fall yesterday. How are you doing today?"

Anissa didn't know how to answer. She just wanted it to go away.

"Yeah," was the first thing that jumped out of her mouth, shoved out by way of the uncomfortable silence that hung, begging for an answer. She felt her ponytail disassembling above her bandage, but it didn't feel right to fix. She couldn't do that casually. She gave in to her disassembling hair, feeling like the favorite porcelain doll of a rambunctious nine-year-old—gone through much more than she was designed to. "Yeah, I'm doing okay. Thanks for asking."

"That's good to hear. Honestly, I'm surprised to see you here today after that. I mean, I'm not sure if I would be after that fall," Ericka said.

What is she getting at? Anissa wondered but tried to hide it. "Yeah, well, not like it'd be much different if I was at home. It'd still hurt."

"I suppose."

Where am I going with this? Ericka thought. She had no idea. She wrung her hands together again, instruments of her own anxiety.

"I have to be honest—I was surprised to get this invite," Anissa said first, hoping to break the ice. Hoping to move on from whatever kind of introduction Ericka was using to procrastinate whatever she was planning on addressing in this meeting. Better to cut straight to the point, and save them both the time.

Usually, that was Ericka's speed, too. But with this, she struggled.

Ericka thought it would be simple to pull the information out of her. She had always been a fan of detective shows, where the detective starts with a shoestring and a bullfrog and leaves with a full-blown, fleshed-out story (and the killer's mother's maiden name, somehow). If only she could start pulling one of those strings. If only she knew where to start without making Anissa suspicious.

"So, you've been getting into a lot of accidents lately. Any idea why that might be?" Ericka began.

Anissa looked back at her blankly. This felt like an interrogation. But for what?

"What are you trying to say?" Anissa said, gauging intent. "I don't think I understand the point of this meeting."

"That came off as strong. Sorry." Ericka wasn't usually one to apologize in a situation unless it was entirely warranted, but she also wasn't one for wasting someone's time.

She felt like she was doing both right now. She had to cut this short. It was clear Anissa didn't know anything about why she was getting hurt. She didn't want to be here. She was actively hurting, and it would probably best for her to return to her desk where there could be Advil or aspirin or something stronger.

"I just wanted to make sure you were okay," Ericka said. "That's all. This is kind of a weird place to work—plus, your fall. I wanted to make sure they weren't related."

"Are you HR, too?" Anissa said with an edge in her voice. She couldn't suppress that edge. She wasn't able to.

"No, no. But I am a coworker," Ericka said.

Anissa moved in her seat, holding her side instinctually to protect herself from another stab of pain. "I mean, kind of. This is the first time we're sitting down together, and I don't think we've ever worked together."

"Yeah, I guess." Ericka sat in her own uncomfortableness. She felt like she was 22 again—as if she were answering to a superior at work when she got their sugar-free double vanilla caramel macchiato order wrong. As if she was being called out. But no, this was different. This time, she might actually deserve it. It was clear Anissa had no idea what was going on. Ericka shifted her tone accordingly. "I just wanted to check in on you is all. It seemed pretty dramatic, and I saw you down there . . ."

"No, I appreciate you checking in. I do. I just want to make sure I'm understanding this meeting correctly. That's it." Anissa could feel the back of her head pounding. She tried to focus on what was happening right in front of her, but she didn't know. She couldn't.

"Just checking in, is all. Let me know if you need anything though, okay? My door is always open." Ericka got up from her chair and opened the conference room door, watching Anissa shift her weight to stand with the least amount of pain as she waited.

They had to be the same age, her and Anissa. Or at least close to it. There's something about that relatability of being in the same generation that makes things tougher in difficult situations like these. If someone two years older than you dies of a heart attack, it hits differently than if someone much older or much younger does. One is an anomaly, one is expected, but that Goldilocks middle hits right in the way-too-relatable zone. The *that could be me* feelings, no matter how different the other person is.

Are we doing the right thing, here? Is all Ericka could think. *If Derrick is up to something, should I help him? Is that the right thing to do?*

Ericka held the door open and waited patiently as Anissa made her way toward it, one belabored foot after another.

Anissa looked elderly, the way she moved. Arched over, frail. Ericka wondered if, because of all the emotional and physical trauma, Anissa was actually aging at a faster rate—if her cell regeneration was slowing as it realized its demise was closer with every accident it endured. It was unnatural what they were doing to her. Keeping her alive like this.

Is Derrick right? Ericka thought. She didn't know if Derrick was planning anything, if Derrick was trying to save Anissa. But something in her gut told her that it was at least on his mind. He would have to be a sociopath if it wasn't on his mind, even if they weren't that close.

Ericka brushed the thought from her head. This was for the best. She had to keep Anissa alive. That was her duty. Her name was in the folder. She must not pass on, under any circumstances. That is what she was told. That is what she would do.

Right?

"Sorry, moving a bit slow today," Anissa said as she finally got to the door.

"God no, you're fine. I could use the break," Ericka said. She used to make this joke with Nathan after his series of accidents, back when she was in Minneapolis. A past life. When she felt the joke leave her lips, she felt her body regressing to that time for a moment, feeling her body go back in time to the oscillating moral grey area, a battle between brain and heart. Back to that point in her life, all too similar to her current situation. "Be careful, though. Be safe. And let me know if there's anything I can do to help."

"I appreciate that," Anissa said, but she wasn't able to make eye contact.

There was something about this meeting that deeply unsettled Anissa. She couldn't put her finger on why she felt so uncomfortable in this moment.

She wanted to walk, to pace, as she'd normally do when she was trying to sort a problem out in her head, but she couldn't. What, in her current state.

She felt her soul did not match her current body, not anymore—like her soul was rattling within this crushed corpus, trying to set itself free.

She hadn't noticed this feeling before, but she was keenly aware of it now.

She saw the chickadee, still hovering by the Death, Inc. entrance. Still waiting behind the glass doors. Still watching her, the sunbeams shining behind it. Everything she wanted was out there, but she couldn't reach it. She couldn't muster up the energy, mental or physical, to put herself in that situation again.

She did her best to ignore it. At least for now.

Chapter 26

B*ing,* rang Derrick's Outlook. Another email from Dennis.

Derrick:
You didn't tell Anissa anything, did you? You didn't tell Ericka anything eithre?

Derrick reviewed it, noting the typo at the end. It was written in a hurry. Quick. Probably triggered by something. He responded.

Dennis:
No, why?

Dennis responded with an invite for lunch—the Outlook location said Applebee's.

Derrick clicked *Yes* on the invite. Not even two seconds later, Dennis knocked on his door.

Was he waiting outside that whole time? Derrick thought, after noting he hadn't heard any footsteps.

***

"Fuck, fuck, fuck," Dennis said as Derrick slid into the passenger's seat of the Buick. When Dennis turned the key, *The White Album* by The Beatles was playing. He turned it down.

"There's no way they know," Derrick said, but his tone was unconfident, unsure. As if he was still trying to convince himself.

“They know,” Dennis said, also with an unconfident yet cautious tone.

“No,” Derrick said, but with an uptilt. It wasn’t a question, but he gave it a questioning tone.

Dennis turned the volume back up on *The White Album.*

“Ob-la-di, ob-la-da, life goes on, brah

La-la, how their life goes on

Yeah ob-la-di—

Dennis switched to the next song. That song always made him feel uncomfortable, but he wasn’t exactly sure why. Something about the tone of it. It just seemed . . .appropriative maybe? But of what, he wasn't exactly certain. All he knew was it was unsettling.

“Wild Honey Pie” was next. He skipped that, too.

Next, in the key of A minor, “While My Guitar Gently Weeps.”

“Now, this—this is a perfect song,” Dennis said, cutting the silence. There was still a bite to his tone, but he made a conscious decision to address that once they got to Applebee’s. It never felt right to argue when the car was moving. It never felt right to argue in a car. A car is a safe space. Tight quarters. You have to give an argument more air to breathe than in a car.

He tried to keep the tone neutral. Derrick appreciated that.

“Yeah, I guess. Have you heard the cover by Martin Luther, in *Across The Universe*?” Derrick asked.

“Oh, no. No. You can’t cover this song. That’s sacrilege,” Dennis assured, then paused before he continued.

“Unless you’re talking about that Tom Petty and Prince version from the Rock and Roll Hall Of Fame induction. That solo? Fucking Prince—now Prince can cover the *hell* out of that song.” He pointed on his steering wheel emphatically with his right pointer finger, pressing the edge of his steering wheel each time he said the last five words of that sentence.

"Martin Luther's—it's pretty good, too," Derrick reiterated. They were arguing about what they weren't saying—music taste, a ready substitute for the conversation they were actively trying to delay.

"I doubt it," Dennis said, without a hint of doubt or pause in his voice.

"I'm sure there are some other covers that are good. It's covered fairly often," Derrick said as Dennis sighed.

Derrick shifted in his seat.

Dennis turned up the last seconds of the song as they pulled into the Applebee's parking lot. They sat there until the song ended, then Dennis turned the car off.

"All right, let's get on with this," Dennis said, pulling his keys from the ignition.

***

The same girl was at front of house, still staring at her phone. Still not giving any sort of shit.

"So, we should just sit anywhere?" Dennis asked.

She looked up and nodded, the bottom half of her face illuminated by her phone as if she were telling a scary story at summer camp. This time, her hair was cut shorter, and she dyed it blue. Or, perhaps it was a wig. Perhaps it was always a wig.

It didn't look bad or anything—Derrick just noted it as he passed her.

This time, she was wearing a name tag. "Allison" was what it said, which seemed like an incongruous name for her, but Derrick couldn't put his finger on why. It didn't seem like her name.

She sighed silently with her shoulders, as she grabbed the menus from underneath the counter ledge. She walked behind them as they chose the booth in the back of the restaurant, closest to the kitchen.

"I'd bet not a lot of people come here around this time. Probably doesn't make a lot of sense, does it?" Dennis said, in Allison's direction, but not to her specifically. She didn't respond. She just placed the menus in front of them.

"Thanks, Allison," Derrick said, but he immediately regretted it. How awkward. Her face finally registered some emotion. He couldn't read it, exactly, but there was something there.

It wasn't a total blank anymore.

She looked up at him, then looked down, as if regressing back into her former self. As if she were buttoning that small emotional release back into her chest.

"Drinks?" she asked.

"Just water would be great," said Dennis, none the wiser. If he had noticed any of this, Derrick would be shocked.

Had I acknowledged her last time I was here? Derrick wondered. *Had anyone ever acknowledged her?*

"I don't think I'm going to get any food, but you're welcome to," Dennis said as he pulled out a sandwich from his jacket pocket.

Well, now I have to get something, Derrick noted to himself. He wasn't about to just get waters and watch Dennis eat a sandwich he brought to an Applebee's.

"They don't care if you don't eat anything. Honestly. They've never said anything. Not a peep."

"I think I'm going to get a burger or something," Derrick said, looking at the menu for the cheapest thing he could find. Maybe $10. Max. "Or maybe an appetizer."

"I could go for some fries," Dennis said.

Derrick put his menu down in front of him, the universal sign for *I have decided what I'm going to order.*

"So, how well do you know Anissa again? You guys know each other before you got this job?" Dennis asked.

"Why?"

"Oh, just curious. It seems like you're doing a lot of heavy lifting for someone who you just met a little over a week ago, is all." Dennis leaned back in his booth cushion and took a bite of his pocket sandwich. It looked like a slice of deli ham between two slices of white bread. That was it.

"I'm not following," Derrick said—and he wasn't filling space, or figuring out how much Dennis knew. He legitimately had no idea what he was talking about. Sure, he had seen Anissa outside of work once, but it's not like it was anything extensive or anything like that.

Dennis shifted in his booth. "She seems to know an awful lot for someone who is supposed to be kept in the dark is all." It was as if he was planning a chessboard, sliding his pawn one step forward.

"What? What does she know?" Derrick asked.

Dennis raised his eyebrow, as if to move his pawn forward once more. Confident.

Derrick countered. "I'm serious. I didn't tell her anything. If she knows anything, it wasn't me."

"So, she doesn't know that she's going to die soon?"

"What? No. How would that come up naturally in a conversation with someone I just met a week ago?"

"So, you two did meet just a week ago. Okay. Well, do you like her or something? You think she's cute? Is there a reason it's so hard to let her go?"

"I'm not used to letting people die, is all." Derrick said this with a sarcastic bite in his tone.

"*Hah*," Dennis said before taking a sip of his water. "I'm just here making sure the natural order is carried out. I'm sorry you're scared of death. I really am. But it's going to happen to all of us eventually. And even when it's my time, someone will be there to guide my soul to its proper place, be it recycling, transcendence, unfinished business, and so on." His tone was dismissive, as if he had repeated it so many times it lost its meaning. Devoid of emotion.

"So that's why you put Christine's soul into a chickadee? Because you are so okay with death and you're so okay with letting her go?"

"That's different," Dennis deflected.

"How?"

"That was for science, to see if it would work. Purely an experiment," Dennis said as he rolled his napkin between his fingers, a nervous habit.

"Only science?" Now Derrick leaned in, moving his pawn forward.

"Okay, okay. You've made your point. I see where you're coming from. Are you happy?" Dennis leaned back in his seat, defeated, arms crossed. "I get it. It's tough," he said, avoiding eye contact.

Allison had been standing at the end of their booth for the past minute, unflinching, still. Derrick didn't notice her until she shifted her weight, and her shoes squeaked slightly, faint.

"Sorry about that. We'll have an order of fries. That will be all for us," Derrick said.

"That's it?" Allison said, eyeing the sandwich in Dennis's hands. Dennis took a bite, as if to challenge her to say something about it.

"Yep, that's it." Derrick tried to apologize with his eyes, trying to say *I realize he shouldn't be doing that, and that is not a reflection on me.* He repressed a *sorry* because that seemed a bit over the top, possibly pedantic. Perhaps she'd pick up on this energy.

Instead, she sighed, not asking whether they'd like a refill on their waters.

Am I making the right move? Derrick thought briefly before Dennis continued their conversation.

"How could the natural order be wrong? It's what is supposed to happen. It's written in the stars already. Or something. Whatever it is. It's preordained, and all we have to do is make sure it goes through. The steps we've added . . . with the processes and machines. And even before Death, Inc. existed, when the funeral industry started using formaldehyde . . . we're already playing with fire as it is. But I guess we can't really go back now, can we?"

Derrick didn't say anything, which Dennis took as doubt.

"It's not like I'm going out there and stabbing people, right? I'm not out there giving people a deadly virus. I'm just helping the soul do what it already knows it needs to do. Like a death doula. I'm just doing what was already set in their cards, preordained."

"So we have a set death date. All of us?"

"Sometimes so, sometimes not. Sometimes, if everything goes 100% according to plan in someone's life, there is a set death date they reach, if they're so fortunate. But sometimes, things go haywire, and the soul is forced to eject before it planned. The process is a bit more abrupt, and a bit more complicated, but overall, the soul decides when it wants to go. We should never try to control what the soul wants to do." Derrick paused, then sipped the water that still lingered between ice cubes, an audible slurp. "Age is a gift that many of us are not fortunate enough to reach. That's not sad. That's just fact."

"To be clear, I'm with you on this particular one, but I'm not sure about everything else," Derrick said. "I agree with you that what's happening now just doesn't seem right, with Anissa."

"I saw Anissa and Ericka talking today," Dennis said quickly.

"What?"

"I said, I saw Anissa and Ericka. You don't know anything about that, do you?"

"No, no not at all. Nothing. I don't know anything about that."

"Really?"

"Really."

Dennis raised his eyebrow again. "But really, though? Did you know anything about this? Absolutely anything? It just seems a bit—" he moved his hands in the air, as if he were trying to grasp a word just beyond his reach.

"Really. I don't know anything. Again, I've just been here for a—"

"Well, you've been here over a week, so that line doesn't work as great anymore." Dennis tipped his glass to rattle the remaining water from between the ice cubes, the melted residue, but he ended up in that awkward ice cubes-all-over-your-face scenario. He placed it down and wiped his face. "But, okay. I hear you. Maybe you didn't know anything. But still. It seems like something's going on there."

"I really doubt it."

"Then how do you explain the meeting?"

"What meeting?"

They both looked at each other.

"You're right. I'm not sure if it was anything official, but they talked in an office for more than 10 minutes." Dennis rubbed his hands through his hair. "Okay, I see it now. I'm overreacting. I'm overthinking. Maybe you had nothing to do with this. Sorry, dude. I'm sorry."

"It's cool, but what did it look—"

"I should have known that you had my back. I should have trusted you. You're a good kid, you know that?"

"Thanks, but what was the—"

"The meeting? No idea. Looked uncomfortable. Couldn't get a good read on it."

Did they know? They'd find out eventually. But finding out before they did anything? A disaster. Fuck, Derrick thought to himself.

"Well, shit. I thought for sure you said something to them. That would have almost been easier." Dennis took another bite of his sandwich. Then, as if it had given him a revelation, he looked back to Derrick and said, "You're sure you said nothing? Like, absolutely nothing?"

"I haven't had time to. I've only been here—"

"You've *got* to stop using that as an excuse, dude. A lot can happen in a week. *Trust* me."

"Well, I haven't. That's the truth." Out of Derrick's periphery, he saw the fries coming. It was as if Allison's face reset. No emotion again, until she looked at Dennis, with his sandwich in his hand. A slight scowl, but for the most part, imperceptible.

"Hell yeah," Dennis said as the fries hit the table.

"Thank you," Derrick said to Allison.

Dennis took the first fry—the longest one. Of *course* he did.

"We've gotta talk about the plan for Anissa. I'm sorry it has to be like this, but we have to let your friend die," he said between bites of fry, as if he were eating a carrot.

"Please stop saying it like that."

"What's wrong about it? Tell me what part of that sentence is wrong."

Derrick couldn't. The feeling of it was wrong, but there's no way to say that without sounding pedantic. Factually, it was accurate. Derrick had to give him that. But something about his tone seemed distant, inauthentic. As if he were speaking through a mask.

"I'm thinking we should do it next week. Kill Anissa, I mean. You're going to have to let Anissa's soul pass on," Dennis insisted.

"But I don't know the door code."

"Oh, that? It's literally *1234*. How could you not know that? Did you even try?"

"I have to reiterate that I've only been here—"

"I know. You've only been here for a week." Dennis took a drink of the last of his water. "Well, now you know. The keypad code is *1234*. Easy peasy. Please don't forget it."

“Sure.” Derrick felt that if he answered as if there had been no hint of sarcasm in Dennis’s voice, that was the best response. Dennis didn’t seem to notice.

Instead, Dennis took another fry.

“So, here’s what we’re going to do. You. You will pass Anissa’s soul on while I distract Ericka. If Harold asks, tell him you’ve got it. He won’t stop you. If he tries, explain to him that it’s really important that you do this one on your own, according to Ericka. He will not pass up the opportunity for less work.” Dennis investigated his cup and rattled it a bit, looking for even one more drop of water. He looked up at Allison, who was on her phone at the front of the restaurant. He sighed.

“I don’t think that’s going to work,” Derrick said. “There’s no way Ericka will take a last-minute meeting with you when a death comes through. She will tell you to wait. She’s. . . particular about that.”

“I’ll come up with something.”

“But I’m not getting the death notifications yet. Ericka’s been forwarding them.”

Dennis sighed a dramatic sigh, as if this was a huge wrench in his plan, but continued as if it was barely an inconvenience. “I’ll email you when I see it. That way, you save your time and only focus on Anissa.”

“That seems like a lot for you to do in the split second it takes Ericka to respond to these things.”

“Watch me.”

"Okay, deal." Yet, Derrick was still unsure. It seemed too simple of a plan to truly work. Could it really be that easy?

The rest of their fry eating was not eventful and naturally deviated to silence, until they finished the basket of fries and Derrick paid. There wasn’t anything more for them to say. They had decided. They knew what they were doing. Now, it was time to act.

Derrick’s phone pinged. A meeting invite.

Dinner with Anissa, 5:30 pm, Applebee’s.

He clicked ***Decline Invite***, with no additional note.

Dennis offered Derrick a ride home, but Derrick chose to walk—he assured him not because he was mad, but because he wanted to clear his mind.

Chapter 27

The next time Anissa nearly died happened the next day, Tuesday, at 2:00 pm.

But, as Derrick had predicted, Ericka was faster than Dennis.

And the uncomfortable thing was Anissa had her near-death experience while falling down the stairs, meaning Ericka had to jump over her lifeless, passed-out body to get to the basement processing room.

To be clear, Ericka wasn't completely heartless about this all. It felt wrong, in all the places it should feel wrong. In the pit of her gut, she felt that, if this were a movie, she would be the clear villain—one the critics would pin as "a bit on the nose, yeah?" But it doesn't really mean much if she felt bad and didn't do anything. That actually makes it worse. That just made her a coward.

Anissa had slipped on someone's ketchup packet. She had been going upstairs to get coffee, the fifth floor, where they had the best hazelnut coffee. She felt a little lightheaded as she was making her ascent. The depression that set in after her initial fall, which gave her a concussion she didn't even know about, made her feel as if she were perpetually waking up—as if she was never truly awake—so she tried to stay awake artificially in hopes that it would go away soon.

She started feeling dizzy, then *wham*. A slippery ketchup packet squished and slicked underneath her $15 Target treadless flats. She hit her wound from two days ago—the gash in the back of the head—which reopened. The edge of the stair— *WHACK*—right on the wound.

There was blood, though it wasn't clear how much—it blended with the ketchup packets into a swirl of different reddish shades and consistencies. Scarlet, ruby, to even a bright cherry where the ketchup exterior remained untarnished by blood.

It was more the bruise on the back of her head that was the problem, though. A second concussion in a span of two days was not excellent, especially when it was on the exact same point of the head. Her poor occipital lobe.

When she came to, Susan was there again, a small crowd gathered around her. New Beginnings had been on their way to lunch, trailing behind Susan as she guided the way to the Applebee's everyone went to.

"Honey, are you okay?" Again, Susan said this more to the crowd than to Anissa.

Anissa couldn't respond at first. It was as if her words were locked right behind her mouth. As if they were behind a plate of glass. She could see them in her mind, but she could not let them out.

She opened her eyes and saw a set of loafers in her face. She recognized those black loafers, down to the scuff on their front.

What were the fucking odds?

She wanted to sigh, but she couldn't. She wiggled her fingers, then her toes. *Phew.* Still could do that. She was not paralyzed. She still had control over her body.

That was always her biggest fear whenever she had an accident like this, or a series of accidents so closely together. While she was sure she would adapt, as many had before, she could not imagine a world where she did not have control and agency over her body. She considered herself strong, but not strong enough to deal with that. She knew people who were, but she knew she was not as strong. A world where she could not communicate was not a world she wanted to be in. In a world where she would have to ask for help, she decided in that moment that she'd prefer suicide.

Somehow, no matter what happened to her, she came out relatively unscathed. As if her body knew how to adapt as long as it remained conscious.

Then, her mouth cooperated.

"I'm fine," Anissa heard herself say, but it sounded far away. Faded. Stretched again. The taffy-like words she heard yesterday returned. Slowed down. She wondered if she was just speaking slowly, but that didn't seem the case.

"She's bleeding—" Susan's words stretched.

"Are you sure that isn't the ketchup?" asked another voice, also stretched.

Susan leaned closer to Anissa's body. Anissa could smell her perfume—an artificial lavender scent, as if someone had sprinkled molasses and unidentified chemicals onto a lavender plant.

"Can you get up, honey? I'm not sure I can lift you," Susan said close to Anissa's face, quiet, though Anissa was sure her words reverberated throughout the halls. Or was that just how her brain was processing them? The taffy-like words again echoed in her brain. "I just got a manicure," she continued.

Anissa nodded as best she could, though her head throbbed. Her body was tired. Heavy.

Could she get up without falling?

She would have to try.

"Let me know if I should get someone, but it might be a minute," she whispered again. She turned to the crowd and proclaimed, "She's okay! She's awake!" to which the crowd cheered, as if this were Susan's doing.

By sheer force, Anissa yet again got herself up, despite a worrying blurred vision and splitting headache. She doubled over, holding onto the railing.

"She's got this!" Susan said, but she couldn't fake the confidence she wanted to exude. There was an unintended lilt to the end of her sentence, as if it were an inquisitive.

"Is there anything you need? Another bandage? Tylenol? Do you need us to call someone?" the voice that asked whether her blood was ketchup asked.

"Don't call an ambulance," Anissa said with a bit too much conviction. The bill. She was not 100% certain this would be workers' compensation, and she didn't want to risk it. She could not handle the pain of this injury and the financial pain an ambulance bill would bring her. "I'll be fine. If someone could follow me downstairs, and get me a coffee, I'd appreciate that." This felt uncomfortable, asking for help—but she feared if someone didn't follow her, she'd be in this same position only a few steps down.

The only thing she feared more than asking for help was her greater fear of actually needing help, permanently.

A man who seemed to sigh out of discomfort more than she was comfortable with, more than she sighed herself, helped her down the stairs. He held the door open for her and said, "Well, back to the old grind," before shutting the door behind her.

Harold figured she could make it to her desk if she made it down the stairs.

He was right.

***

On Ericka's side, everything went as usual.

Usual, in that she wondered if what she was doing was the right thing. If she had gotten too callous in the places she should remain soft—the places that allow humans to stay human.

If, maybe, this job wasn't worth it if it were to turn her into someone who would continue to lie on every date she went on, would continue to question whether protocol was the right call.

Give it a night to think it over, she thought to herself, as she did every time this thought crowded her head. Every time for the past five years.

Chapter 28

"Shit, you're right—she *is* fast."

Dennis did not announce himself when he arrived in Derrick's office. Derrick didn't hear Dennis open the door, nor did he hear his footsteps. Or anything. It had been surprisingly dead quiet, outside of a thud he heard from the stairwell.

"What?"

"I mean Ericka. She's quick as hell, isn't she?"

"Oh." Derrick suddenly processed. The *thud* he heard a moment before. Ericka. Anissa. "Right."

"She's tough as hell. Anissa, I mean."

"Yeah, maybe," Derrick thought, but he couldn't get himself out of what may have happened in the stairwell. *What the fuck just happened to Anissa?*

"It was a fall. She fell on a ketchup packet," Dennis laughed, but it seemed misplaced. Like a laugh track in a horror movie. "Probably for the best she survived that, right? How embarrassing."

"Yeah, maybe," Derrick said again. But he wasn't listening. He could only imagine what had happened, imagined her pain, her humiliation, her inner torment. He ran his fingers through his hair. "Well, what should we do next?"

"Well, it's only going to continue to speed up as her soul keeps trying to leave. It happens to everything that tries to cheat death. Death doesn't like that."

“Death?”

“To be clear, death is not a person. It's just—well, an inevitable force, outside of us. Think of death like a computer program that keeps restarting. Like in the movie *Final Destination*. It will keep going until it’s either able to complete, when the soul leaves the body permanently, or until it’s forced dormant. So for Anissa, that would be a coma. It’ll keep going in quicker succession until she’s either dead or in a coma.”

“I don’t understand,” Derrick said, more so because of the horrific nature of Dennis’s statement and not that he wasn’t understanding. Does a coma appease death? How could that be right? *That can’t be right.*

“Or at least, that’s what I’ve heard. I’ve never seen it happen, but that’s what they say. About comas, I mean. Not all, but some.” Dennis coughed. “Anyway. It’s only been a day since her last death. I’m guessing it will probably be tomorrow morning, at this rate. Can you get in early?”

“How early?”

Dennis paused as if he were doing math in his head, a mental abacus.

“8:00 am?”

“I’ll already be here.”

“Even better.”

***

Dennis was right—the next morning, it happened.

This time was even more embarrassing than the last.

It was a curb. She tripped over a curb right by the Death, Inc. entrance.

Luckily, Gary was still there when she fell. And luckily, she hit the front of her head this time, not the back. Right in her forehead, lightly, before her hands caught the rest of the fall. It was a damned miracle she didn't break her jaw or her nose. Her forehead broke the fall.

And this time, Dennis distracted Ericka with something. He told her he needed help moving his desk. Something that would physically keep her from looking at any of her devices while still being putsy enough to take as much time as he wanted.

"I think it should be a little to the left, yeah?" Dennis said as he looked at Ericka from his left periphery. "I just don't want to be in the position to have to move it again."

Ericka didn't respond. She only hooked her fingers underneath the edge of the heavy oak L-shaped desk and dragged it slightly to the left.

"I'm sorry, other left. I meant the right. One day, I'll know my rights from my lefts. How embarrassing!" Dennis said, paired with a fake laugh. He looked down at his phone. The death came in. He forwarded the message to Derrick. Derrick sent back a thumbs up emoji. He was on it.

He heard Derrick's door shut, then the stairwell door shut.

So did Ericka, but she didn't think anything of it.

***

Is this the right thing to do? Derrick thought. It seemed right this morning, and when he was falling asleep last night, and when he thought about it the other dozen times since he found out—what was it, only four days ago?

How could this much happen in such little time?

No time to think about that now.

He was already at the third floor, as if his thoughts warped his speed. He tried to focus as he went down the remaining three floors, to the basement.

It's just going to keep happening. You need to do this now, before it gets too serious, he thought, cringing at his own thought after it appeared in his mind.

1-2-3-4. His fingers pushed the buttons as if he had done it a million times, though this was his first. Autopilot, guided by adrenaline.

In his back-left pocket, he had the notes he took the first time Ericka brought him down here. The folders.

But it was smudged.

Fuck.

He had a vague idea of what he needed to do, but the smudges. . .

It's amazing how a process can seem so obvious when you're taking it in, but as soon as the guide is gone, you're shot. When the spotlight is on you, all logic evaporates. And then, you're on your own.

Derrick has never been great at confidence under stress. When shit hit the fan, he usually let others take the lead as he processed from afar. A flaw of his—one he readily admitted, but now had to face it head-on.

Focus, Derrick, he thought to himself.

It starts with the first machine, the one with the receipt paper dangling out of the register on the top.

Start with that. He ripped that off. First folder. Time for the first folder.

He knew what to do with the first folder. It was simple. All he had to do was match the number on the receipt to the number in the folder, then match it to the name.

He already knew the name, but he hoped if he followed the steps verbatim, it would all come back to him. Kind of like riding a bike, except if your only experience with a bike was to see someone else riding it twice before thinking, "Yeah, fuck it—I don't need training wheels."

Breathe in. Breathe out. Anissa Fontaine.

What a great name, Derrick thought to himself. *What an absolutely perfect name.*

Focus. *Breathe in. Breathe out.*

He picked up the second folder. He looked for Anissa Fontaine. Anissa . . . Anissa . . .

He found her on the third page.

You've got this, Derrick.

He tried to push aside the reality of what he was doing, and surprisingly, it was simple. He was sure it would hit him later. But when he wasn't looking the consequences dead in the face, with that necessary distance, he was able to at least pretend in the meantime.

Right?

He got Anissa's Soul Signifying Number. He walked over to the machine.

Could it really be this simple? Was this what he was worried about? How could he forget a process so simple, so basic?

He typed *9-5-1-5-3.*

But instead of the machine printing out another sheet—

ERROR.

That was all it said.

Fuck. What?

He tried to enter it again.

The machine started beeping.

He looked for a cord—anything that he could unplug. Anything he could do to make it restart. Anything. A fresh start.

But there was no cord. Nothing.

How does this thing run? Derrick thought to himself. *Batteries?*

No time. *Breathe in, breathe out.*

How is it still beeping?

He looked at the number again: *9-1-5-5-3.*

Fuck.

Off by one number. Of fucking course.

He could feel his hands starting to shake, a clammy sweat forming in his palms. They had never told him about what happened now. They never thought to. There was no reason to.

That's when he saw Harold's face.

There was no knock—just the top of Harold's red forehead as Harold looked down to enter the keycode and opened the door.

"Having a little trouble here?" Harold asked, his arms folded loosely across his chest. It was difficult to tell if he was mad or if he was uncomfortable.

Derrick didn't know how to ask, so he said, "Yeah, I figured I'd help out while Ericka is busy. I didn't think it would be this hard to do."

"It is. It's a lot harder than you'd think, isn't it? A lot of people think our job is easy. It just isn't." Harold paused, as if he were addressing something Derrick was not privy to.

"Mind showing me where you're at so I can help you out?" Harold said as he walked toward the second machine, which was still beeping *ERROR*. Derrick tried to see what Harold was doing, but by the way his body was positioned, it was difficult to tell. There was something on the side of the machine—he could see that. It looked like he pressed three buttons, but when Derrick had looked around the machine, he saw nothing on its side. He tried to look over Harold's shoulder, but by the time he got it, there was nothing to see.

"Oh, okay. I see where you're at. Okay. Yep. I see now. You're lucky this wrong number wasn't another soul number. Whew. Passing on the wrong soul is no good. Whew. No good."

Derrick handed Harold the number. Anissa's number. Harold was about to enter it, before he had a physical revelation.

"I'm just going to double check this real quick here, just to make sure this isn't one of the *do not pass. Do not pass go*, if you know what I mean." Harold continued to riff as he opened up the second folder, but Derrick wasn't listening. At this point, he couldn't. He was concentrated on focusing his energy into willing Harold to miss Anissa's number. Into not seeing it at all.

"Oh, wow. Derrick. You are lucky this didn't go through. Boy, are you lucky! Beginner's luck is right!" Harold held the number up as he closed the fourth folder. "This is Anissa. We don't pass Anissa on. Luckily, her soul will just reabsorb back in, like nothing happened, but don't tell Ericka about this little snafu, okay? She does not like when this happens."

Derrick played dumb. "Do not pass on? Why not?"

"Not sure. Never asked. Just know we're not supposed to, is all." Harold checked the number one more time before he tossed the number in the trash.

"And also, not a word of this to Dennis, okay? About the "do not pass on"s. He thinks we're processing them all through."

"Why can't we tell Dennis?" Derrick asked, feigning innocence.

"Oh, boy. He would NOT like this," Harold said. "A real stickler for the rules, that guy. Never got it myself." He let out a little laugh. "Next time, just check the fourth folder, okay? We cannot pass these people on for a reason, even if that reason may not be clear to us. This is our rule, just not his. But our rules are more important than his, okay? He just can't know about it."

"Got it," Derrick said, noting that next time, he should be more careful when entering the number.

"I'm not saying our rules are more important, to be clear. I'm just saying they're different, and it's difficult to explain to him why we do the things we do, is all. Best to keep it quiet."

If Harold wasn't so *Harold-y*, this may have sounded like something out of an old mafia movie. With Harold, however, Derrick knew that's *just the way it was*. For a while.

Chapter 29

Anissa gasped for breath on the concrete step near the front entrance of Death, Inc.

"FUCK. Thank God," Gary said. "I was just about to start doing CPR . . . and I don't even know how to do that."

"Is anyone else here? Did anyone else see?" Anissa asked, anxious.

". . . I don't think that should be your biggest concern right now. Are you okay? How do you feel?"

"I just want to be sure nobody but you saw that."

"I mean, I don't think so. Nobody that I saw."

"Phew."

"Do you want me to take you to a doctor? What is this—four head injuries in one week? Christ, Anissa, maybe you should have someone check you out before getting back to work."

"I can't afford it."

"I'll help—Christ, it's not that big of a deal. I'd rather have you better."

"Not worth it. It's just going to happen again, Gary."

"But Anissa—"

"Trust me."

He looked at her for a moment, and saw her eyes were clear. Connected. He paused, thought, then continued. "Okay, okay. You know best. Sure. But you call me if anything feels off, okay? We're worried about you."

"I appreciate that, really. But I'm fine."

Gary held out his hand to help her up. Anissa took it and pulled herself up, trying to suppress a grimace from the pain that shot through her side as her muscles strained around her bruised ribs. Anissa smiled through it, and Gary gave her a suspicious side glance.

"I'm fine, Gary. I've dealt with a lot worse," Anissa said. But she really wasn't sure of that. Not anymore. These falls, these "accidents"—these were now happening in rapid succession, as if something was actively mad that she wasn't dead. As if something was playing Whac-A-Mole with her. As if every time she stood up, she'd be dodging a mallet.

At this point, she was tired. At this point, she didn't see the point of trying to fight it. The next time she fell, she wanted it to be the last time.

And it wasn't that she was suicidal. That wasn't it at all. She loved what her life had been before.

It wasn't even a dramatically made decision in her head. Just final. She wouldn't do anything actively. She wouldn't actively put herself in harm's way. But if something happened?

A small part of her had wanted it to be over the first time she fell in Colorado, when she was whitewater rafting and watched her boyfriend's limp body smash over and over between granite boulders that, just the day before, they had marveled at. That part of her grew with each accident, as each recovery got more intensive than the last, as more injuries piled up.

It was more that she was so tired now. Always so tired.

And she'd read that concussions can do that—can make you depressed, a mechanism the brain uses to force you to stay in bed and recover—but that wasn't practical in today's world, especially at the rate she was going. She didn't have time to rest. She didn't have time to sleep. She had to support herself. What good was sleep and recovery if she couldn't afford the food necessary to nourish and supplement that recovery?

"Okay. I'll pick you up at 5, okay? But let me know if you need anything today. You. . . you don't seem great right now."

"I appreciate it."

Gary looked at Anissa as if to say *are you sure?* one last time. Anissa responded with a look of *please stop—it's unnecessary*.

She thought she was thinking logically. There was no other way to explain it, but it felt like her time. Deep in her chest, she felt like she had overstayed her welcome.

She knew it was her time months ago, and thought she was mistaken then. But with each accident, she became more certain she'd overstayed her welcome. She had even gotten a will drafted, for what little she had. She didn't have much, but she didn't want to make it even more complicated than it already had to be.

But now. Now, she felt like an intruder. As if she had cheated something. As if she were a glitch. An accidental survivor, one that slipped through the mortal cracks over and over and over.

Could it be the concussions? No. This was too clear of a revelation.

Why was she still here? What was keeping her here?

***

She has to know by now, Derrick thought. *She has to know. There is no way she doesn't know by now.*

"Fuck, what happened?" Dennis said, in an explosive whisper.

"I forgot something," Derrick said as he continued to look at the scrap of paper on his desk, trying to fill in smudges he still had blank.

But that wasn't the problem he had. The problem had been the typo. It wasn't that he had forgotten the process. It was that he fucked it up from negligence. He was going too quickly.

No amount of breathing in or breathing out or meditation could calm his trembling hands.

"You forgot what?" Dennis asked, furious.

"More of a typo."

"Shit." Dennis ran his hands through his hair, visibly stressed, then looked back up to Derrick. "Do they know?"

"No," Derrick said a bit too quickly. Corrected himself. *Slow down.* "Harold got the notification on his email and came down to help me. There's no way he knew."

"Are you sure?"

"We can never be 100% sure of anything," Derrick felt the words slip out of his mouth, the 100% wrong words he tried to pull back as soon as they came out.

"What the fuck does that mean?" Dennis said. He ran his hands through his hair, again. Repeatedly. Not casually, but a nervous tick. His hair stood straight up when he stopped, and he held his hands up to emphasize the words as he said them. "They ! can!not ! know !", a pause between each syllable.

Derrick regrouped. "I just meant that there's never a 100% certainty in anything."

"Nope. No. Nope. Now is not the time for that. We do not need a philosophical exercise right now. I just need to know the situation. No ponderings." Dennis paced the floor, pulled up a chair, sat down, stood back up, and sighed, "She's probably going to die again tonight. There is no way she will make it through sleeping on that head without something happening. No fucking way."

"So, how should we proceed?"

"You're going to have to stay here tonight."

"That's not happening."

"Excuse me?"

"I can't tonight. I have plans," Derrick lied.

"No, you don't," Dennis said, saving time. Derrick is a transparent liar.

Derrick didn't correct him.

"I have a cot in my office if you want to use it, but whatever you think is best. But we *have* to do this tonight."

"Why so urgent?"

"Derrick. I think we both know how we got here today. This should be over by now."

"I've only been here—"

"You've been here longer than a week, Derrick, and I think I've kept you up to speed on anything. That excuse is really running out of steam."

"I have to go home and grab a few things."

"I have a spare toothbrush and all your basic toiletries in there. You should have everything you need."

"I have to water my fern."

"It'll survive one night."

Derrick wasn't sure why he wanted more time. At this point, he knew exactly what would happen if he didn't do this tonight. He knew that it would keep happening if he didn't do something tonight. The clear right answer is to end it tonight.

"Unless you want to see her in a coma, you're going to need to do this tonight. You can't start dating someone when they're in a coma."

"I'm not into her like that, it's just—"

"Or whatever your motive is. Whatever it is. Whether it's friends or something more. At this point, it's selfish."

Derrick thought of Anissa in a coma, tied to a bed with an intricate series of tubes. Eyes empty, body breathing. A coma he knew she'd never exit, even if she had the best doctors in the world at her bedside.

Fuck, he's right.

"Okay. Let's do this tonight."

Chapter 30

Like most things in life, the things that are built up the most often end the least dramatically, wisping away as your adrenaline soars.

Such was the case with Anissa's death. Like the old T.S. Eliot quote, *not with a bang but with a whimper*—you know the one.

It was more the waiting that wrung on Derrick's heart. The anticipation versus the follow-through. The text from Dennis saying, "It's time" felt like a relief rather than the prick on his heart that he thought it would be.

He had been preparing for this so long—well, relatively speaking. Conflicted, yes. He didn't know her well, and he was more fascinated by her and the potential of friendship than any sort of attachment. But that doesn't negate the feeling, the underlying sadness he felt as his face grew resolute.

Again, he had only been here for a little over one week. But in this week, Derrick went through more moral trials than most go through in a lifetime.

Was he truly doing the right thing—allowing the soul to pass on as it was trying to, not intervening as he'd been instructed to by Ericka and Harold?

Derrick went downstairs, the eight floors he's become so familiar in descending. He brought his guide, still smudged, but with notes on top of it. He had filled it in later, when his adrenaline subsided and his memory returned. It wasn't as complicated as it seemed, after all.

And now, his adrenaline was low. Surprisingly low.

He typed in the door's code: *1-2-3-4*.

He looked at the machine. He heard it whirring—the sound of an old fax machine on its last leg. He saw the receipt.

Step 1. Step 2. Step 3. Step 4. He paused before he entered her Soul Signifying Number into the second machine. He thought of the way she seemed to put everyone at ease. How important she must be to someone. At least *someone.*

But then he snapped out of it. *This was for the best.*

9-1-5-5-3.

“This is for the best,” he said to himself, out loud.

He double-checked the number.

“This is for the best,” Dennis texted him, uncharacteristically. He was certain Derrick would be struggling right now. That he might be second-guessing.

Dennis sent a second text. “And please don’t fuck it up this time.”

He wasn’t going to fuck it up. For once in his life, he wasn’t going to fuck it up.

He didn’t.

***

Meanwhile, Anissa was asleep in a Murphy Bed in Gary and Stephanie’s spare bedroom. She did not register that she died. All she felt was peace.

Earlier that night, she cleaned up her room and left her things in order, which was unlike her. It was as if she knew instinctively that this was coming tonight, unlike the other times. Like a wolf who distances himself from the pack when he’s sick. Like a deer who retreats further into the woods after she’s been injured. Like many of us will say, “Don’t worry about me, I’ve had a good life,” right before our final natural breath, Anissa cleaned her room and folded the burnt orange cardigan she wore that day, setting it carefully on the dresser against the wall next to her.

Death, Inc.
142 Goulding Ave, Schuester, IL
October 25, 2022
Derrick McNamara
Marketing Intern

Dear Derrick,

Your employment with Death, Inc. is terminated, effective immediately.

Due to irreparable negligence resulting in the untimely demise of a protected individual, we have decided to terminate your position.

If you have taken anything home with you, please return to the front desk ASAP. We will send all necessary termination paperwork to the address listed on your hiring paperwork.

Please let us know if there is anything you need from us in the meantime.

Respectfully,
Harold Whittier
Death, Inc. CEO, Schuester Branch

PS: If you could please turn in your article by the end of the week, we would appreciate it. Even if it's just a draft.

Dennis Smith
Schuester, IL
October 25, 2022

Dear Derrick McNamara,

Dennis Smith, LLC. is pleased to offer you employment as a 1099 independent contractor in accordance with the terms below:

I. POSITION.
(a) Title: Executive Assistant
(b) Duties: Discussed at time of employment

II. TERMS.
(a) Supervisor: Dennis Smith
(b) Start Date: 10/25/22
(c) End Date: ☒ Indefinite ☐[DATE]
(d) Minimum Hours: 40 hours per week
(e) Pay: $25 ☐per Project ☒ per Hour ☐ Commission ☐[OTHER]

III. CONDITIONS.
(a) Acceptance. Contractor must accept this offer by 10/25/22.
(b) Background Report Required? ☐ Yes ☒ No

If the above-mentioned terms and conditions meet your qualifications for your services, it would be our pleasure to work with you. Please accept our offer by contacting me at any of the following methods:

Phone: 555-555-7812 | Email: dennis@deathinc.com

We happily look forward to the opportunity of working with you.

Sincerely,
Dennis Smith

I, Derrick McNamara, hereby agree to the terms of the above offer of employment. I understand that this offer is non-binding with a separate agreement to be written afterward.

Contractor's Signature: ________________________________ *Date:* ________________________________

Print Name: Derrick McNamara

Chapter 31

Derrick had expected these two forms—the termination letter and the offer letter—but he did not expect the call he received shortly after.

"Is this Derrick?" a woman's voice said as soon as Derrick picked up his phone, before he could even say *hello.* Her voice was certain, not asking. She knew who she was speaking to.

"This is he," Derrick cleared his throat, moving away from the sputtering Mr. Coffee in his kitchen so it wouldn't interrupt. "May I ask who's calling?"

She didn't answer his question. "I'd like to thank you for your work yesterday. As I'm sure you know, things were getting a bit . . . well, unpredictable. You used impeccable judgment in an unprecedented situation." He could hear the sound of birds from the speaker, as if she were outside or perhaps in the middle of an aviary.

"I'm not sure I'm following," he said, sitting down on a peeling La-Z-Boy in his studio apartment's living room area. The morning sun cut in a blade across his grey carpet.

"As the creator of the list you went against, I think I can say with more certainty than most that you've done good work. She knew too much to continue, and you handled it admirably. I will take care of it now." She paused, but before Derrick could ask more questions, she continued. "It is my understanding that you've been let go from Death, Inc. Schuester. If you'd like, I believe I have an opportunity you'd be a great fit for, starting immediately, if you're willing to relocate."

There was a coldness to her tone—knowing, yet unwilling to divulge more than absolutely necessary.

"I've actually accepted another position, but I appreciate the offer," Derrick's gut stretched. Her voice was controlled, yes, but there was something else there. Something . . .

"I understand. Be in touch if you ever change your mind, or if things don't work out with Dennis. Goodbye, Derrick." *Click.*

***

All she could hear were birds. Loud, yet muted, as if she were in a cavern filled with millions of chirps but she was underneath a tarp.

At first, she thought she left her window open the night before—a group of tufted titmice lived in a bush outside of her window, and they were often loud in the morning.

But as she came to, she realized she was wet, all over. A thick wetness. As if her entire body was surrounded by phlegm. She tried to open her eyes, but she couldn't. She stretched her body, but she found herself trapped inside . . . something. She felt its walls, round. Ovular.

She pushed against the walls, repeatedly. At first, they didn't give. They seemed impenetrable until finally, she felt a crack. Freedom, then a breeze. She continued to stretch her limbs, repeatedly bashing against the walls until she broke free completely. The birds grew louder as she continued to crack through this, wherever it was.

What the hell . . . she tried to say to herself. But when she tried to form the words, she couldn't, as if her tongue and lips had been replaced with different tools. Narrow. No teeth. Long. Her voice, too, sounded different. Higher.

She stretched her limbs, then bent, then stretched them again. Not right. They didn't bend right. As if someone had disassembled her, then reassembled her too hastily.

Then, she heard footsteps. Loud. She could feel the earth shaking beneath her as they crescendoed toward her. Slow. Methodical, yet approaching, until finally, they stopped.

"Welcome home, Anissa," a woman's voice said. "We've been expecting you."

***

To be continued.

Thank you to my wonderful editor, Jessica Pearse. I have no idea how I'd publish anything without you, and it feels unfair that I'm not crediting you as a co-author sometimes. As I say to anyone who will listen—you're my forever editor.

Thank you to my spectacular beta readers, specifically Steve Salerno, David Kaye, Liz D'Alessio, Kevin Petitt-Scantling, and Caroline Somsen. (Here's an excellent time to mention if you agreed to be a beta reader but didn't have time to finish—it's okay!! It is not your fault!! I'm terrible at time management and gave it to you all way too late!!)

To Lion's Tooth, the bookshop where I feel most comfortable writing. To Sugar Maple, the bar where I feel the most comfortable relaxing. Both were equally important in completing this project.

To my friends, my family, and anyone else who has supported me through this creative process. I appreciate you more than you know.

To my writing group. You all inspire me to be a better writer and a better person. You rule!

www.ingramcontent.com/pod-product-compliance
Lightning Source LLC
LaVergne TN
LVHW100528110826
845146LV00002B/818

* 9 7 9 8 9 8 7 5 5 3 5 2 7 *